D0036378

MANDIE
AND THE
SHIPBOARD
MYSTERY

Mandie Mysteries

———

Mandie's Cookbook

MANDIE
AND THE
SHIPBOARD
MYSTERY

Lois Gladys Leppard

BETHANY HOUSE PUBLISHERS
MINNEAPOLIS, MINNESOTA 55438

Mandie and the Shipboard Mystery
Lois Gladys Leppard

Library of Congress Catalog Card Number 90-080010

ISBN 1-55661-120-X

Published by Bethany House Publishers
A Ministry of Bethany Fellowship, Inc.
6820 Auto Club Road, Minneapolis, Minnesota 55438

Printed in the United States of America

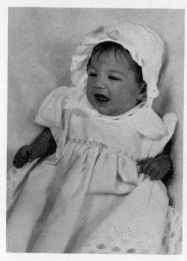

Photo by Bill Sentell.

For a very special Mandie,
who arrived 4:55 A.M., December 26, 1989
at 475 Table Rock Road, Cleveland, S.C.,

AMANDA ELIZABETH SMITH,

great-great-granddaughter of the
first Amanda Elizabeth.

About the Author

LOIS GLADYS LEPPARD has been a Federal Civil Service employee in various countries around the world. She makes her home in Greenville, South Carolina.

The stories of her own mother's childhood are the basis for many of the incidents incorporated in this series.

Contents

"Let not mercy and truth forsake thee:
bind them about thy neck;
write them upon the table of thine heart"
Proverbs 3:3

Chapter 1 / The Send-off

Mandie's blue eyes grew wide with excitement as the buggy came to a halt in front of a huge mansion in downtown Charleston, South Carolina. Sitting behind the driver with her friends Joe and Celia, Mandie's heart beat faster as the driver hopped down and swung open the heavy gate in the surrounding high brick wall.

Mandie turned and grinned at her mother, grandmother, and Uncle John in the seat behind her. "Here we are!" she announced, stroking her white kitten, Snowball, in her lap.

Mandie had visited Tommy Patton before with her mother and stepfather, Uncle John, but this would be a much shorter stay. The next day Mandie would set sail for Europe with Celia, Grandmother Taft, and Grandmother's friend Senator Morton!

The driver jumped back into the buggy and drove down the narrow driveway toward the impressive three-story brick house surrounded by beautiful trees, shrubbery, and flowers in bloom everywhere.

Joe half stood and stared at the mansion. "You mean those Pattons actually live here in this huge building?"

Celia fanned herself in the July heat. "It's beautiful!" she exclaimed.

"This is the Pattons' *town* house," Mandie explained, smoothing the thick blonde braid that hung down her back.

As the vehicle came to a stop, a uniformed servant walked from the house to help with the baggage.

Mandie and her friends jumped down onto the stone walkway. "They also have a house at the beach and that huge plantation, Mossy Manor, where we visited last year," she continued, tightening her grip on her squirming kitten.

After John Shaw helped his wife and mother-in-law from the buggy, he turned to the young people. "I'm sure you will all enjoy our visit here," he said.

Elizabeth laid her hands on her daughter's shoulders. "Now I want all three of you to conduct yourselves in an exemplary manner while we are guests of the Pattons," she reminded them.

"Yes, ma'am," the three chimed.

Grandmother Taft patted her faded blonde hair into place. "And remember," she added, "Senator Morton should be here already, so I know y'all will want to be well behaved."

"Yes, ma'am," the three said again.

As they headed up the front steps, Joe nudged Mandie. "Thank goodness we only have to spend one night in this big old mansion," he said.

Mandie frowned at him and was about to say something when Tizzy, the Pattons' downstairs maid, greeted them at the front door. Tizzy's eleven-year-old daughter, Cheechee, instantly appeared beside her, grabbed Snowball from Mandie, and ran off, promising to feed him. Mandie smiled, remembering how much Cheechee had enjoyed playing with the kitten on their other visit. With

Cheechee in charge of Snowball, Mandie knew she probably wouldn't see much of her kitten until they sailed.

Tizzy ushered them into the hallway. "De Pattons, dey all be home any minute now," she said. "Y'all come on in. Dat Mistuh Senator Morton he be waitin' fo' y'all in de drawin' room."

Mandie watched Joe's reaction as he gazed around the marble-floored entry hall. A marble staircase rose out of sight into the stories above. Gold and silver sparkled everywhere. Velvet and silk draped the windows and upholstered the chairs. Old portraits lined the wallpapered walls.

"Oh, Mandie," Celia cried, "everything is so pretty!"

"Uh-huh," Joe said, running his long fingers through his unruly brown hair.

Mandie's blue eyes twinkled with excitement. "Come on," she urged her friends. "Wait till you see the rest!" She led the way, following the adults to the huge, ornate door of the drawing room.

Just inside the doorway Joe and Celia again stopped to stare. The room looked as though it belonged in a palace. The heavy expensive furniture was upholstered in a peach-and-gray silk brocade, and the draperies were a darker shade of gray with golden tassels. The young people's heels sank into the thick carpet, which covered most of the parquet floor. Joe and Celia stood silent in wonder.

Across the room Senator Morton sat near an open French door beside the huge gray stone fireplace that covered almost the entire wall.

Mrs. Taft led the visitors into the drawing room, and as soon as the senator saw her, he stood and grinned broadly.

"Senator Morton." Mrs. Taft crossed the room quickly and greeted him with obvious delight. "It's so nice to see you again."

Mandie nudged Celia. "Grandmother's in a hurry to see the senator," she whispered. The two girls stifled a giggle.

The older gentleman bowed slightly. "My pleasure, dear lady," he said. "I look forward to your company on board ship." Then he turned to say hello to Mandie and Joe, whom he had met at President McKinley's inauguration earlier that year. "Miss Amanda, and Joe, so nice to see you again. Joe, are you sailing with us, too?"

Joe shook the senator's hand. "No, sir, I'm afraid not," he replied.

After Mandie introduced Celia, and Mrs. Taft made the other introductions, they all found places to sit.

Tizzy stood at the doorway, waiting for a break in the conversation. "Excuse me, ma'am," she said, walking over to Elizabeth. "Miz Patton, she say fo' me to serve tea when you gits heah and dat she oughta be heah shortly thereafter."

"Thanks, Tizzy, that would be nice," Elizabeth told her.

Tizzy hurried off and the guests began discussing the forthcoming voyage to Europe. Mandie, Celia, and Mrs. Taft had been planning this trip for quite some time, and coincidentally Senator Morton was planning a similar trip.

"I'm so excited, I won't be able to sleep tonight," Mandie said. "It's going to be a wonderful adventure."

"I'll say it will," Joe said sarcastically. "Knowing you, you'll probably get lost over there with all those foreigners and never find your way home again."

"Oh, Joe!" Mandie exclaimed. "How can we get lost when we have Grandmother and Senator Morton with us? They've both been to Europe several times. Between them I'm sure they know everything we need to know over there."

"Well, don't go poking your nose into things," Joe warned. "Remember, I won't be there to get you out of trouble."

"I don't need you to get me out of trouble," Mandie said. She caught her mother's eye and knew the adults were listening to her conversation. She lowered her voice. "My mother thinks I'm old enough now to take care of myself. Grandmother will be with me, so Mother agreed it wasn't necessary for Uncle Ned to go."

Just as she said his name, she looked up and saw her old Indian friend standing in the doorway. She gasped. "Uncle Ned! I didn't know you were coming!" Running to him, she took him by the hand and led him into the room.

The adults exchanged greetings.

In spite of her joy at seeing her old friend, Mandie looked at Elizabeth, confused. "Mother, you said Uncle Ned wasn't going with us."

"No, he is not going with you, dear," Elizabeth explained. "But he will be here to see you off tomorrow."

Mandie smiled at her dear friend who was always watching over her—ever since her father died. "I'm glad you came, Uncle Ned, so you can see the huge boat we're going on."

The old Indian patted her head. "Biggest, finest boat in Charleston Harbor."

Sitting near Mandie, Uncle Ned began visiting with everyone. Soon the Pattons arrived home, and the parlor was full of people and happy conversation.

Mandie's friend Tommy Patton rushed over to greet her. She had met Tommy when the girls' boarding school she went to in Asheville, North Carolina, got together with the boys' school he attended.

"Mandie, I know you and Celia must both be really excited," he said, sitting on a stool near them. His sister Josephine stood by silently, watching and listening.

Tommy turned to Joe. "I'm sorry you don't get to go," he said. "Maybe you could spend a few days with us here, and we could show you the beach."

Joe frowned. "No, I'll be going back on the train with Mr. and Mrs. Shaw, thank you," he said coldly.

Tommy seemed puzzled at Joe's unfriendliness. "Then maybe you could come visit some other time when the Shaws come," he offered.

Tizzy brought in a fancy tea cart, and Mrs. Patton began serving tea and tiny iced cookies to her guests.

Mandie felt the awkwardness between the two boys. She had first met Tommy Patton at a tea at her school. Then they had discovered that their parents were old friends, and the Shaws spent a vacation with the Pattons the year before, in 1900.

Mandie knew Joe was jealous of Tommy, but she didn't understand it. Tommy wasn't any better looking than Joe. He was just a lot taller, more polite, and wore nicer clothes.

Joe was her lifelong friend from back in Charley Gap, where she had lived with her father until he died. Tall and thin, with intelligent brown eyes, he was overly protective of her. Although she was only thirteen and he wouldn't be fifteen until November, he took it for granted that Mandie would marry him when they grew up. Mandie felt she was too young to be tied down with a promise of anything so far in the future.

Without enthusiasm Joe thanked Tommy for his invitation to visit again.

Mandie looked up to see Josephine, Tommy's sister, staring down at her through her wire-rimmed eyeglasses. Skinny and almost as tall as her brother, Josephine had long brown hair. She brushed it behind her ears and dropped onto a chair near the settee where the young people were sitting. "Where is that new baby brother of yours I heard about, Mandie?" she asked.

"At home," Mandie replied. "The trip all the way from Franklin, North Carolina is too long for a little baby."

"What about your friend Hilda who lives with your grandmother?" Josephine persisted. "Didn't you want her along?"

Mandie struggled to control her impatience. "Grandmother left her with her next-door neighbor until we get back from Europe," she explained. "And before you inquire about everyone else, I'll run over the list. Celia's mother had business to attend to and could not make the trip from Richmond. Joe's parents, Dr. and Mrs. Woodard, couldn't come because the doctor had calls to make. I think that covers everyone, don't you?"

Josephine didn't answer for a moment, then leaned forward and glanced toward the adults across the room. "Is that senator sweet on your grandmother?" she asked.

Mandie could feel her face turning red from anger, but before she could answer, Tommy lashed out at his sister.

"Josephine! Please remember your manners," he said firmly.

Celia held her hand over her smile, and Joe turned his head, obviously trying to hide his grin.

Josephine sighed loudly, jumped up, and hurried out of the room with a limp—left over from an old foot injury.

Mandie tried to break the tension. "Tommy, could we show Celia and Joe the widow's walk?"

"I was just going to suggest that," Tommy answered.

"Oh yes!" Celia cried, smoothing her long auburn curls. "Mandie told me about it after her last visit."

Tommy turned to Joe. "Want to go?"

"Sure. Why not?" Joe stood up.

Tommy led the way to the third floor, and there he opened the door to a small room. Inside, a narrow spiral staircase led to the roof.

Celia looked up the steps. "Scary!" she exclaimed.

"Just don't look down from up there," Mandie cautioned.

Tommy stood to one side. "You girls go first, and Joe and I will be right behind you in case you slip or anything," he said.

With the boys following, the girls cautiously made their way up the narrow steps, never daring to look down. They stopped at a small landing at the top, and Tommy reached past them to take a key from a nail on the wall. With this he opened a small door in front of them. As the door swung open, Celia gasped.

Mandie grabbed her friend's hand. "I know it's frightening," Mandie told her. "It looks like there's nothing but sky out there."

"Come on," Tommy urged.

They all stepped through the doorway onto a narrow walkway that ran around the edge of the roof.

Mandie gripped Celia's hand tightly. "Remember I told you that back in the old days the wives would have come up here to watch for their husbands' ships to come in?"

Celia nodded, but her fear showed plainly on her face. "That must have been hard not knowing when ... or if ... their husbands would come home," she said.

Tommy pointed out to the harbor. "Look over that way," he said. "See all the ships?"

Between the Pattons' house and the harbor were dozens of beautiful homes, and palm trees lined the avenues. But gazing out beyond at the harbor, the young people talked excitedly about the many ships crowding around the docks.

"Is the ship y'all are sailing on down there?" Joe asked.

Mandie turned to Tommy. "We're going on the *Queen Victoria*," she said. "Do you see it?"

"I don't see a Union Jack flying on any ship down there," Tommy replied, "but then I believe I heard my father say it wouldn't dock here until late tonight."

"Union Jack?" Celia looked puzzled.

"It's a British ship, so it'll have the British flag on it," Tommy explained.

"Of course." Celia nodded. "Dumb of me. I knew that, but you know this will be the first time in my life I've ever actually traveled on a ship."

Tommy smiled broadly. "Not dumb, just inexperienced, right Joe?"

Joe shrugged. "I fall into that inexperienced category," he said. "I've never even been near a ship before. It must be great to be rich enough to travel all over the world."

Before anyone could answer, there was a sudden rustle behind them. They all whirled around to find Tommy's sister standing there.

"Celia," Josephine said, walking toward them, "did Tommy tell you about Melissa Patton? She was killed up here, you know."

Celia gasped and Mandie shot Josephine an angry look.

Tommy scowled at his sister. "Josephine, don't start that again," he scolded.

"But that's part of the history of this house," Josephine said, leaning over the railing. "Melissa Patton fell or was pushed over right here, and she splattered all over the flower garden below."

"Ugh!" Celia shuddered.

Tommy lifted his hand as though he were going to strike his sister, but she was too quick for him. She ducked through the doorway and disappeared down the stairwell.

Mandie turned to Celia. "She likes to tell people that the ghost of Melissa Patton walks around up here when there's a full moon, too," Mandie said with a laugh. "Josephine lives in a dream world, Celia. You can't believe much of anything she says."

Joe frowned at Tommy. "Is that really so? Was it one of your ancestors who was killed up here?"

"It's an old, old tale," Tommy explained. "The rumor is that she either committed suicide by jumping off the roof here or else she was pushed. Anyhow, no one ever knew whether it was just a ghost story or whether it really happened."

Mandie changed the subject. "Tommy, let's go down and look at the flowers in your yard," she suggested.

Tommy agreed and the young people followed as he led them downstairs and out through the beautiful flower gardens. Then he gave them a tour of the mansion. By that time dinner was ready in the huge, elegant dining room.

At the incredibly long table—Mandie thought a hundred people could be seated there—Mrs. Patton seated Mandie next to Tommy, with Joe across from them between Uncle Ned and Celia. Mandie could tell by the look on Joe's face that he was jealous. He obviously didn't like Mrs. Patton's arrangement, assuring that her son had Mandie's attention.

Everyone was grouped around one end of the huge table so that they could converse easily during dinner. Of course the forthcoming journey to Europe was the main topic of conversation as they began their meal.

"Amanda," Elizabeth caught her daughter's attention. "You need to get to bed early tonight so you'll be fresh tomorrow," she said, touching her napkin to her lips.

"Yes, Mother," Mandie replied. "But I know I won't sleep a wink all night."

Mrs. Taft leaned forward and looked down the table at her granddaughter. "Even if you can't, you will be able to take a nap anytime you want after we sail tomorrow," she said.

Mandie set down her fork. "I'm so excited I can hardly eat."

Uncle John laughed. "I'm sure you'll eat if you get hungry enough."

Celia, who had been practically gobbling down her food, looked up. "I don't understand why Mandie can't eat. All this excitement makes me so hungry I could just about eat everything. I hope they have lots of good food on the ship."

"You can be sure they will," Mrs. Taft told her. "We'll all probably gain ten pounds, don't you think, Senator?"

"I certainly hope not." Senator Morton laughed.

Mandie could hardly keep from laughing herself. Senator Morton was so thin he could stand to gain ten pounds. "I just wish all of you could go with us," she said, looking around the table.

Tommy set down his water glass. "We're all going on board, you know."

Celia's eyes grew wide. "You are?"

"Yes, to wish you all a *bon voyage*," Tommy explained. "That's the custom when someone is going on such a long journey. It's like a party."

Mandie frowned. "What if the ship starts sailing before you all get off?"

"The captain always warns everyone," Tommy assured her.

At last Joe broke his long silence. "It would be funny if everyone got stuck on the ship and had to go to Europe, wouldn't it?"

Tommy shrugged. "Not really."

Mandie shuddered at the thought. She didn't want Uncle Ned and her mother and Uncle John on board to "watch over her." She didn't need their supervision. Grandmother would look after her and Celia. Yet she secretly hoped her grandmother would be preoccupied with Senator Morton so that she and Celia could do things on their own.

That night when they went to bed, Mandie and Celia were given separate rooms. But since there was a door between their rooms, Celia soon came to climb into Mandie's bed, and they talked into the wee hours of the morning with Snowball sound asleep at their feet. Neither of the girls was sleepy, but they did doze a little before the Pattons' maid woke them for an early breakfast.

The girls jumped out of bed and danced about the room. A startled Snowball sat up in the middle of the covers and stared at them.

"It's today! It's today! We're leaving today!" Mandie exclaimed, running to the open window. "And the sun is shining. This is going to be the best day of my life." She stopped suddenly and added, "Almost."

The girls settled down and sat on the bed.

"Right." Celia nodded. "I know the best day was when you found your real mother."

"You're right," Mandie agreed. "That was the most wonderful day I've ever experienced."

"Mandie, do you think we'll get just a little homesick, being gone so long from home?" Celia wondered.

Mandie instantly perked up. "Oh no, Celia." She laughed. "We won't get homesick. We'll be too busy sightseeing. Besides, we stay away from home longer than two months when we're at school in Asheville."

"That's true. But I'm glad we'll at least have your grandmother with us," Celia replied. "You know we're going to be in the middle of no one but foreigners."

"That's just the fun of it!" Mandie reminded her. She jumped up and reached for the dress she had worn the night before. "Let's get ready and hurry downstairs to eat. I can't wait to get going."

Celia looked puzzled as Mandie pulled the dress over her head. "Are you wearing that again?" she asked.

Mandie nodded. "Remember Mother said we weren't to unpack anything from our bags except what we wear to board the ship," she reminded her friend. "I'm certainly not wearing my traveling suit to breakfast. Besides, all our trunks are already down at the dock, waiting to be loaded onto the ship."

"That's right, I forgot," Celia gave in, slipping into her own dress from the previous night. "We'll have to come back up here and change into our traveling suits just before we leave."

Helping each other to dress quickly and fix their hair, they hurried downstairs to find everyone else already in the breakfast room. The girls seated themselves at the only two remaining places—next to Josephine. Mandie rolled her eyes and Celia nodded. Two maids came and began serving them a delicious-smelling breakfast of sausage, eggs, and grits.

Everyone talked excitedly about the journey except

Joe, who sat between Tommy and Uncle Ned across the table from the girls. Mandie tried to get his attention, but he stared down at his plate with a glum expression and picked at his food.

"We must hurry, Amanda," Elizabeth prompted her daughter. "The ship docked late last night, and we can go aboard within the next hour."

Mandie took a quick sip of her coffee. "What time does it sail, Mother?" she asked excitedly.

"Probably around noontime," Elizabeth sounded uncertain. She looked to John Shaw for confirmation.

"That's right," Uncle John agreed. "It's scheduled to leave at noon. We'll go aboard with you all and stay until the visitors have to leave."

Uncle Ned leaned across the table and patted Mandie's hand. "Papoose, me not go ship. Papoose and me have powwow. Then say goodbye."

Mandie's shoulders drooped. "Oh, Uncle Ned, I thought you came here to see us off," she said.

"Eat. Then we talk," the old Indian replied. Cutting a sausage with his knife, he took a bite.

Mandie and Celia exchanged glances, then began eating hurriedly.

Josephine leaned across Celia to talk to Mandie in a hushed tone. "Are y'all so poor you have to wear the same dresses you had on last night?"

Tommy bristled. Before Mandie or Celia could answer, he leaned forward and spoke quietly to his sister. "If you say another word, I'll speak loud enough so that Mother will know what is going on."

Josephine straightened up and began eating her eggs.

Mandie couldn't let Josephine's remark pass without

comment. "We have to hurry through breakfast, Tommy," she said loudly enough for all to hear, "because Celia and I have to go back upstairs and put on our traveling suits. Oh, wait till you see them, Tommy. Mine is a beautiful blue and Celia's is green. We have trunks just running over with new clothes."

She took a deep breath before continuing. "Grandmother took us to Raleigh to shop before we left. She said we wouldn't have time to buy anything here in Charleston, and I guess she was right." She smiled at Tommy.

Tommy smiled back, obviously understanding why Mandie had to get out all this information.

When they had all finished eating, Uncle Ned left the table, and Mandie followed him out onto the wide veranda. They both sat down.

"Uncle Ned, I wish you could go to the ship with us," Mandie said sadly.

"Business important. Not go to ship." The old Indian leaned forward and looked into her blue eyes. "Papoose must promise be good. Old Ned not there to watch." He smiled and his weathered face folded into a thousand wrinkles.

"I promise to be good, Uncle Ned," Mandie replied. "But you know I am thirteen years old now, and Mother has even given Celia and me permission to pin our hair up, so you see, we've grown into young ladies." She reached for his old wrinkled hand and squeezed it tightly. "But I do love you, Uncle Ned, and of course I'll miss you, too."

"Remember, obey grandmother. Mother not there, so grandmother boss," he reminded her. "Remember, thank Big God every day. Think first everything. No secret adventures. No slipping off from grandmother. Behave like young ladies." His eyes twinkled.

Mandie gazed into his loving face. "I promise, Uncle

Ned," she agreed. "I promise to behave. You know I really am going to miss you."

The old Indian stood up. "I go now." Starting for the steps down to the yard, he stopped and turned back. "Papoose behave like Jim Shaw would want." With a smile he hurried down the walkway into the street.

Mandie sat there quietly for a minute, thinking about their brief, strange conversation. He didn't say he would see her again, and that was always the last thing he said when they parted. And he mentioned her dear father. Before Jim Shaw died, Uncle Ned promised him that he would watch over Mandie. He had been there for Mandie ever since, rescuing her from one mess after another.

Now she was going all the way across the ocean without Uncle Ned. She had told him she was old enough to take care of herself, but she shivered a little at the idea of being so far from his protection. Shaking the thought from her mind, she hurried inside to find Celia so they could get dressed and go down to the ship.

Uncle Ned would be back home in North Carolina when she got there.

Chapter 2 / Anchors Aweigh!

The Pattons had to harness their small rig as well as the larger one in order to hold all the people and baggage. The six adults rode in the small rig while the young people piled into the other one amid all the baggage. Mandie had to hold Snowball tightly because he squirmed fiercely to get down.

As the buggies started off, Mandie rode silently, wishing Uncle Ned could have come to see them off.

But Josephine talked constantly all the way to the wharf. "If you watch long enough, you can see ships from every nation in the world dock here," she said. "And someday when I am older, I want to ride on every one of them. I want to go to Holland and see the people wearing wooden shoes, and to Italy to see all the famous fountains, and to Greece to see the Acropolis, and to Africa to see all the wild animals."

The others ignored her, almost dozing in the warm sun.

Josephine pushed her glasses up on her nose. "And then I'd just love to go to wherever it is those women do that bellydancing."

Suddenly she had everyone's attention.

"Josephine!" Tommy scolded. "How vulgar!"

"But there really are women who dance with their bellies somehow," she insisted. "I've read about it but I just can't remember where—"

"Well, when you learn how they do it," Joe interrupted, "you'll just have to show us how it's done," he said with a grin.

"Joe!" Mandie exclaimed.

"Sure, Joe. I'll be glad to." Josephine glanced at Mandie to watch her reaction.

Mandie tightened her lips and said nothing.

Celia leaned forward. "Mandie, do you suppose there are any of these dancers where we're going in Europe?" she asked.

"You know as well as I do that Grandmother would never permit us to see such a thing," Mandie answered. "But I doubt that the people of Europe do it anyway."

A short time later, the driver of the small rig stopped ahead of them on the road leading to the dock. As soon as their rig stopped, the young people jumped down, and Snowball almost struggled free.

"Look!" Mandie exclaimed. "There's the *Queen Victoria*! Isn't it beautiful?"

Celia stared at the huge ship. "Tommy, I do see the Union Jack flying up there," she said.

The others just stood there for a moment, watching as the ship's gangplank was lowered and people walked up and down, to and from the ship. There were several other large ships at dock, but the *Queen Victoria* was the most luxurious.

The adults looked back, waiting for the young people to join them. "Amanda," Elizabeth called.

"Oh yes, Mother." Mandie felt the spell of excitement broken. "We're coming." Securing Snowball tightly, she rushed ahead with her friends and quickly caught up with the adults.

A man in uniform at the foot of the gangplank checked everyone through, and they all walked up the steep incline toward the ship's deck.

Celia grabbed Mandie's hand. "This is really high and scary," she said.

Mandie stopped for a moment with her friend. "I'm sorry, Celia," she replied. "I know you are afraid of heights."

Joe came up behind Celia and took her arm. "I'll hold on to you," he offered. The three walked up the gang-plank together.

As they reached the rail at the top, another uniformed man directed them to the proper deck. The girls oohed and aahed as they followed through the elegant interior of the ship.

Senator Morton took charge and found the reserved cabins. Ahead of them, he stopped in front of a door and pushed it open. "I believe you have number 12A, Mrs. Taft. This is it." He turned to Mandie. "And you young ladies have the adjoining cabin, which is number 14A."

He walked into the room ahead of them and tried to open the connecting door. "It's locked," he said. "We'll have to get someone to open it. Now my cabin is number 13A, which is right across the hall from these two."

The girls and Joe wandered around Mrs. Taft's room, looking at all the beautiful furnishings—all velvet and silk. None of the three had ever been on a ship before. Leaving Josephine with the adults to talk, they took Tommy with them to explore Mandie and Celia's cabin.

Mandie shoved Snowball inside a tiny closet and shut the door so she wouldn't have to worry about her kitten running off. "Sorry, Snowball," she said. "I'll let you out when we're done exploring."

"Look!" Celia cried. "Two beds—one stacked on top of the other."

Tommy smiled. "They call them bunks on a ship," he said.

"Mandie," Celia began slowly, "would you by any chance prefer the top one?"

Mandie laughed. "Of course, Celia. I don't mind, but don't blame me if I fall out during the night and wake you up!"

Tommy stepped forward. "See the rails up there?" Pulling a sliding board out from the foot and head of the bed, he fastened them for Mandie. "Now, that will hold you in."

"Great!" Mandie exclaimed. "Thanks, Tommy." As she gazed around the room, she spotted the porthole in the wall and walked over to look out. "Celia, we're on the outside of the ship," she said. "You can see right out onto the deck. Look here!"

Celia joined her and peered through the round window.

Tommy turned to Joe. "Too bad we can't go, too, to watch out for these girls," he said with a smile.

Joe shuffled his feet. "Nah. I don't really want to go," he said. "Later maybe, when I'm older. I'd like to see the world, but not now."

"Maybe when I'm older I'll go again," Tommy replied.

Josephine popped her head in the doorway. "I've been on a ship before, but I was too small to really remember anything much," she said, coming into the room. "So I can't wait to travel."

At that moment the connecting door swung open, and a man in a red-and-gold uniform stood there. Behind him the young people could see into Mrs. Taft's cabin, which was full of people now.

"Must be friends who came to say goodbye," Tommy said.

Josephine craned her neck to see what was going on. "Hey, I see food in there." Pushing her way through the crowd, she disappeared into the other room.

"There's food all right," Tommy affirmed. "See those carts covered with white tablecloths? Let's get something."

Mandie and Celia sipped on lemonade and awkwardly stood listening to the adults' conversation. Tommy, Joe, and Josephine were not so shy, and helped themselves to the delicacies.

Mandie nudged Celia. "That man holding the newspapers and talking to Senator Morton—didn't we see him at the White House when we went to President McKinley's inauguration?"

Celia followed her gaze and nodded. "He does look vaguely familiar, but I don't remember exactly where we saw him."

The girls watched as the man handed the stack of newspapers to the senator. "I brought you all the latest newspapers," the man said. "I thought maybe you'd like to read them sometime during your journey."

Senator Morton laid the papers on a nearby table. "How thoughtful of you. Thank you."

"His voice sounds familiar, too," Mandie said. "Oh, I remember now. He sat next to Senator Morton at the President's dinner that night. I suppose he's just a friend of the senator's."

Celia looked around the crowded cabin. "All these people . . ." she said. "It's a good thing that man unlocked the door between the two rooms."

Mandie nodded and suddenly realized that Joe was standing beside her.

"Excuse me, could I talk to you a minute, Mandie?"

"Sure." Mandie didn't move.

"Not in all this crowd," he said.

Mandie looked at him in surprise.

"Let's walk out into the hallway for a minute," Joe suggested. After excusing themselves, Mandie followed as Joe led her through the clusters of people and out of the cabin.

When they reached a cross hall on the other side of Mrs. Taft's cabin, Joe leaned against the safety rail on the wall and cleared his throat a bit nervously. "Mandie, I just wanted—" He paused and ran his long, thin fingers through his hair, making it more unruly than ever. "I just—" He stopped.

Mandie looked at him curiously. It wasn't like Joe to be at a loss for words. "I'm listening," she assured him.

Joe reached out, put his hands on Mandie's shoulders, and spoke quickly, as if to get it over with. "Mandie, I just wanted to say that I'm going to miss you, and I'll be wishing the days away until you come back." He blushed slightly.

Mandie smiled. "That's the sweetest thing you ever said to me, Joe," she said. "I really appreciate it. And I'm going to miss you, too."

"I wish you didn't have to be away so long," Joe said. "I'll be so worried about you, being on this great ship out in the ocean in the middle of nowhere, and in strange countries where you don't know anyone."

Mandie looked into his sad brown eyes. "But Grandmother knows people in Europe," she reminded him.
"She's been there lots of times, and she knows her way
around. So don't worry about us. We'll be all right."

"I'd feel a lot better about your safety if Uncle Ned
were going with you," Joe insisted.

Mandie pulled herself up as tall as she could manage.
"Joe Woodard, I'll have you know that I don't need anyone
hovering over me. Remember I was thirteen last month,
and my mother agreed that I didn't need Uncle Ned
along."

"She agreed after several arguments," Joe reminded
her. Then softening his voice, he said, "Let's not quarrel,
Mandie. It's not worth it. Please?"

Mandie smiled and her blue eyes brightened. "I'm
sorry, Joe. I don't want to quarrel either." She paused for
a moment and then said, "Joe, will you wave to me from
the wharf when the boat pulls out? I'll be at the railing."

"Of course, Mandie." Grinning, he reached for her
hand and squeezed it. "I was already planning on it."

As soon as the captain called for all visitors to leave
the ship, Mandie and Celia hurried to get a place at the
railing to wave goodbye to everyone.

Celia gazed out over the mass of people on shore.
"This ship is so big, and we're so far up in the air, I can't
tell who anyone is down there."

The ship lurched, blew off steam, and sounded its
horn.

"Oh, that gives me goosebumps." Mandie laughed.
She clung to the rail, squinting to see Joe on the dock.

Suddenly a huge white flag rose out of the crowd.
Mandie caught her breath. "Look, Celia!" she exclaimed.
"That flag says, 'Hurry Back, Mandie.'" She shaded her

eyes for a better view. "And that's Joe holding it." She waved her handkerchief and quickly threw a kiss.

Celia looked at her and grinned.

"I wonder where he had that flag," Mandie said. "Maybe he hid it in the other buggy." She pondered the question as the huge ship slowly pulled farther and farther away from shore.

The girls waved until the people on shore were mere specks, then they started back to their cabin to get settled. Mrs. Taft and Senator Morton were standing right behind them.

"Grandmother, I wondered where you were," Mandie mumbled, realizing that her grandmother had seen the flag. For some reason she wished others hadn't seen it.

"I've been right here all along," Mrs. Taft said, smiling. "And so has the senator. But now we're going to stroll around the deck. Don't get lost now, you two. And remember, we will be at the first seating for dinner tonight. So be ready at precisely seven o'clock." She started to leave, then turned back. "And girls, do dress formally. We're sitting with the captain!"

"Yes, Grandmother," Mandie answered, smiling at her friend. This was going to be such an exciting trip. "Come on, Celia. Let's get out of some of these hot clothes and shed our bonnets. I think we should do some exploring."

"Are you remembering Snowball? He must be suffocating by now, shut up in that closet," Celia commented.

"Oh, my, yes! Celia, thanks," Mandie said as they hurried toward their cabin. "I clear forgot."

When Mandie opened the closet door to free her kitten, she was surprised to find him curled up, sound asleep.

"Come on, Snowball, you can come out now," Mandie whispered. "You can stay in our room while we walk around outside. I'll take you out for some fresh air later."

"We'd better latch the door to your grandmother's room, so she won't open it and let him out," Celia cautioned.

"You're right," Mandie agreed. She quickly closed the connecting door and latched it.

Snowball stretched and then explored the room, sniffing at everything. The girls shed the jackets to their traveling suits and removed their bonnets.

"Whew!" Mandie exclaimed, smoothing back her blonde hair, which was pinned up on top of her head. "What a relief to get those things off."

Celia stood in front of the long mirror on the door and adjusted the bow on her lacy blouse. "I agree," she replied. She straightened her ankle-length skirt.

Suddenly the ship gave a lurch again, throwing the girls off their feet. A knock sounded at their door.

Mandie gasped. "What's going on?" Regaining her balance, she went to answer the door.

A good-looking young man in a red-and-white uniform smiled at her through the doorway. "Hello, miss, I am just checking to be sure everything is all right." He had curly black hair, blue eyes, and perfect white teeth.

His British accent was so thick Mandie could hardly understand him. "My name is Charles," he said. "I will be your steward for this journey."

Mandie tried to close the door a little as she reached with her foot and pushed Snowball behind her. "Oh, everything is fine," Mandie told him. Celia looked out over her shoulder.

"If there is anything you need, I'll be glad to get it for you," Charles told her.

"Nothing right now, thank you," Mandie replied.

"At any rate, I shall be stationed at the end of this corridor," he gestured down the hall. He gave a nod and turned crisply to continue down the hallway.

Mandie closed the door quickly and turned to Celia. "Did you see him? Wasn't he good looking?"

"Yes! I noticed too," Celia agreed. "Do you think we'll be needing anything soon we could ask him for?"

Mandie smiled. "I don't understand exactly what his job is, or what he can get for us, but I think we ought to find out."

"Me too." Celia grinned.

"Come on, let's look this ship over," Mandie said. She pushed her kitten away from the door before opening it. "Sorry, Snowball, but you'll have plenty of room to roam around in here while we're out."

The girls slipped out onto the windy deck and headed in the opposite direction from which they'd come on board. As the ship rocked with the big waves, they made a game of catching hold of the railing to regain their balance.

"I didn't realize a ship as big as this one would rock like this," Mandie said, clutching the rail.

"I've heard about it," Celia commented as they walked on. "In fact, a lot of people get seasick."

"Seasick?"

"Yes, you know, you get dizzy and can't keep your food. . . ."

Mandie moaned. "Oh, how awful! I hope that doesn't happen to us."

"They say that if you don't get sick within the first day or two, you'll be all right for the rest of the journey," Celia explained.

As they continued on around the deck, they passed several gentlemen in red-and-white uniforms. Rows of deck chairs lined the open spaces. They even noticed a drinking fountain in a small recess of the ship. The lifeboats lining the railing of the deck made Mandie feel safe.

The ship lurched again, and the girls headed for the rail. But the wind was strong, and the girls had to hold on to each other to make it to the railing. As Celia peered out over the ocean, she quickly backed off.

"Oh, dear. I can't look down there," she protested. Turning back, she headed for a chair. "Let's sit down a minute. It's too windy to walk anyway."

Mandie agreed, and indicated two vacant deck chairs away from the railing.

As the wind whipped around them, Mandie reached up and felt for the tortoise-shell combs she had used to pin up her long, blonde hair. "Oh, I think my hair is falling down," she cried. She tried to anchor the combs again.

"Mine, too," Celia said, shielding the auburn curls on top of her head from the wind.

"Celia, look around," Mandie whispered. "Everyone else is wearing a bonnet. I guess we'll have to wear ours if we want to keep our hair from blowing around."

They watched as other young girls and older ladies walked past them. Not a single one was without a bonnet, and most of them were wearing jackets too.

"Oh, well," Celia sighed. "We're out here now. We can put ours on next time."

Mandie gazed out at the endless ocean and the distant horizon. "Look, Celia," she said. "There's nothing but water. Not a speck of land in sight. Makes you feel weird, doesn't it?"

Celia nodded solemnly. "Like being in another world."

Mandie glanced around, then quickly looked back at Celia. "Don't look to our right, but we're being stared at."

Celia turned her head only slightly. "By whom?" she asked.

"A little old lady. I've never seen her before," Mandie replied under her breath.

Celia stood. "Let's stroll again so I can see her. We should get our bonnets too, don't you think?"

"Fine, but go to your right, and we'll pass directly in front of her," Mandie instructed. "She's sitting in a chair up against the wall about fifteen feet away." As the girls walked past, Mandie tried to avoid the woman's gaze.

Although she was dressed in expensive clothes, nothing seemed to fit the woman quite right. She wore a fashionable bonnet, but wisps of untidy gray hair stuck out in various places. The sunlight reflected off the many diamonds adorning her skinny fingers, and an enormous brooch decorated the neck of her black dress.

Her black eyes riveted on the girls as they walked by, and even when Celia glanced her way, she didn't move her head.

"Did you see her?" Mandie whispered after they'd passed the woman.

"Uh-huh," Celia replied. She glanced backward a second. "And she's still staring at us."

"Well, she ought to know us the next time she sees us," Mandie said with a grin.

"It's kinda scary," Celia replied.

Chapter 3 / The Strange Woman

When the girls finally got back to their cabin, they opened the door to find a large cut-glass bowl full of fruit on the little table in the corner.

"Look! Somebody's brought us some fruit," Celia said.

Mandie looked around the room suspiciously. "And hung up our clothes in the closet," she added.

Snowball rubbed around his mistress's legs and purred.

"I wonder who it was," Mandie puzzled. "It was probably the senator who brought the fruit, don't you think? And Grandmother must have found a maid to unpack."

"Maybe, but the fruit sure looks tempting." Celia picked up a bright red apple, then put it back. "It must be getting near suppertime."

"My stomach would agree with that," Mandie sighed. "Let's just stay here and rest until it's time for supper, all right?"

Celia lay down on the lower bunk. "Remember your grandmother said we have to get dressed up," she reminded her. "By the way, I really appreciate your taking the upper berth, Mandie."

Mandie climbed the ladder and asked Celia to hand Snowball up to her. While Mandie stretched out on the bed, the kitten meowed and pranced around, uneasy with the height.

"Snowball," Mandie fussed, "don't tell me you're afraid of sleeping up here." She caught him and cuddled him close. "I won't let you fall off."

All the excitement and fresh air had tired the girls, and they'd almost dozed off when they heard someone at their door.

Mandie raised up on one elbow to see the door open slowly. A face peeked through the opening, and Mandie quickly climbed down the ladder. "What is it?" she demanded, crossing quickly to the door as someone closed it. Then with a jerk it came open again. She almost fell back, but Celia was right behind her and caught her. Both girls stared.

There in the doorway was the strange woman who had been watching them on the deck. Obviously flustered at being caught, she stammered, "I . . . I must have the wrong cabin." Turning quickly, she hurried down the corridor and the girls saw her disappear around the corner as they looked after her.

Mandie and Celia stood watching a moment, but she didn't come back, so they closed the door and sat down on the small settee in their cabin.

Mandie frowned. "I really wonder who that woman is," she said thoughtfully.

"Why would she be snooping on us?" Celia asked. "Maybe we should tell your grandmother about her."

"Oh no, Celia. We can't do that," Mandie objected. "Why, Grandmother wouldn't let us out of her sight if she knew someone was following us around. Let's just start watching her."

"How are we going to do that?" Celia wondered aloud. "We don't even know what cabin is hers."

"Hey!" Mandie jumped up. "Maybe that Charles fellow would know who she is. He'd at least know which is her cabin. Let's go find him. He said he's stationed at the end of this corridor. Come on."

Celia followed her friend out the door and down the hallway. At the end of the corridor they found a small recessed area with a tiny counter and a stool, but no one was there. A bell with a sign:

RING FOR SERVICE

sat on the counter, but there was no one in sight.

"Well!" Mandie sighed in disappointment.

Celia looked around. "He told us he'd be here if we needed anything."

"Maybe he had to go on an errand," Mandie replied. "I'm sure he must be busy serving other guests. Let's go down this other hallway and look for him." She started toward the cross hall.

Celia caught her sleeve. "Mandie, isn't it about time to get dressed for dinner? It's going to take me forever to get ready because I'm not used to wearing my hair up like this."

"I guess you're right," Mandie agreed. "We sure don't want to be late for dinner. There's no telling what Grandmother would do if we were late at the captain's table." They turned and headed back to their cabin.

They looked through the expensive dresses hanging in their closet. Celia's mother had bought her daughter a whole new wardrobe for the journey, and Mandie's grandmother had almost done the same, even though she had bought Mandie a number of new dresses for their trip to Washington D.C. earlier in the year.

Mandie shook her head. "I'm going to feel awfully silly in one of these fancy long gowns," she complained. "I don't understand why we have to get so dressed up and be so uncomfortable when all we're going to do is eat supper."

"But Mandie, that's the custom," Celia explained. "I know that much from my mother. She says when you're traveling a long distance onboard ship you are expected to wear formal clothing for dinner every night. And it *is* dinner in the evening, not supper, as we call it."

She finally selected a yellow satin dress and carefully removed it from the hanger. "I don't like these fancy things any more than you do, but we have to follow custom if we're going to take this journey."

"Maybe you and I should just start another custom while we're on this ship," Mandie said with a grin.

Celia looked shocked. "No, Mandie, no!" she protested. "We can't upset your grandmother. She'd tell our mothers for sure, and that would be the end of our adventures."

Mandie sighed heavily and took down the first dress her hand touched. "Well, maybe they'll make it all worthwhile and have something good to eat." She unbuttoned the bodice of her traveling suit and let it drop to the floor.

Celia smiled at the thought. "Maybe we'll see that good-looking Charles at dinner."

"There's a good possibility," Mandie smiled. "And you know that strange woman has to eat sometime—maybe she'll be at the first seating tonight, too," she said. "Then we can ask around to see if anyone knows who she is." Standing before the long mirror on the door, Mandie straightened the long skirt of her baby blue dress.

Celia turned her back to Mandie and asked her to finish buttoning her dress. "I don't know why they make dresses with so many buttons in the back where you can't reach them," she fussed.

"Oh, but they're pearl buttons, Celia," Mandie said, fastening them one by one. "They really make the dress look elegant, and you look especially pretty in yellow with your auburn curls. There," she said, fastening the last one. "Now what are we going to do with our hair?"

Celia thought a moment. "How about threading my pearl necklace through my hair instead of wearing it around my neck? It would look special, wouldn't it?"

"Yes. And I'll just use a few of these rhinestone combs in mine," Mandie decided. She tentatively placed one in her hair and then added three more to secure her blonde tresses.

The girls were ready, but they'd heard nothing from Mrs. Taft's room.

"Maybe we should see if Grandmother is getting ready," Mandie suggested, knocking on the connecting door.

There was no answer, so she unlatched it and opened it carefully. No one was in the room.

Mandie turned to Celia. "Didn't she say we were to be ready for dinner at seven o'clock?" She flipped open the pendant watch hanging around her neck. "It's fifteen minutes to seven right now."

Just at that moment, Mrs. Taft's hallway door opened and she came hurrying into her room. "Oh, dear, oh dear," she muttered. "I can't be late." Then she noticed the girls, and stopped suddenly, putting a hand to her face. "My, but you both look like princesses!"

"Thank you, Mrs. Taft," Celia replied.

"Now you girls can wait for me in your cabin, I'll be ready in just a few minutes."

"Of course, Grandmother," Mandie said, leaving the room with Celia. She closed the door and twirled around in her long blue gown. "Well, I wonder what held *her* up till the last minute?"

"Senator Morton?" Celia said with a grin. She mimicked Mandie's elegant twirling movements.

Mandie stopped suddenly and stared at her friend. "You're right. I think my grandmother is what you would call 'smitten' with the gentleman," she said. "But I'm glad, because I really like the senator."

"I like him, too, Mandie," her friend replied. "Do you think he might ask your grandmother to marry him?"

"Marry him? Well, I don't know about that." Mandie thoughtfully patted her hairdo. She smiled. "But, that's not such a bad idea, Celia, because then I'd have a grandpa, wouldn't I?"

"A step-grandfather, Mandie. Not a real one," Celia corrected. "There's a difference."

"Since my two real grandfathers died before I was ever born, I think it would be nice to have the senator for my very own grandpa," Mandie decided.

Celia frowned. "Do you suppose he has any children or grandchildren of his own?" she asked. "Because if he has, they might not want to share him with you."

"Oh, Celia, that's silly," Mandie teased. "What difference could it make to them if I claimed him, too? I do know my grandmother must like him an awful lot, because they were together everywhere in Washington, D.C., remember?"

"That's right."

"And he must like my grandmother," Mandie continued. "In fact, I think he came on this journey just because of her." She looked around the room. "I wish Grandmother would hurry. I'm tired of standing, and if I sit, I'll wrinkle my dress before dinner."

"Lean against the wall like this," Celia demonstrated.

But within seconds Mrs. Taft opened the door between the rooms. "Be sure you close the door now, dears, so Snowball can't come into my room. He might decide to sleep on my clothes there." She indicated a pile of dresses on hangers lying across the bed. "I don't have time to hang them up," she added, a little embarrassed.

Mandie and Celia looked at each other and grinned as they closed the connecting door.

As they followed Mrs. Taft out of their room, Mandie whispered, "I guess she couldn't make up her mind what to wear."

Celia nodded.

Senator Morton was waiting for them in the corridor, and taking Mrs. Taft's arm, he led the way to dinner.

At the doorway of the dining room, the girls stopped and stared. The room was huge. There must have been hundreds of tables covered with white linen tablecloths and set with fine silver, delicate china, and sparkling crystal. Waiters in formal attire stood ready, and the smell of food made Mandie ravenous.

In the center of the room on a raised platform a uniformed orchestra was softly playing a waltz.

A man with a dark complexion, who was dressed in evening clothes, stood at the entrance taking names and telling other employees where to seat the guests. But when he came to them, he spoke to the senator briefly, then escorted them personally to the captain's table.

Captain Montrose stood, greeting the dozen people

who would dine with him that evening around a large round table. He was a tall, slender man with gray hair and a huge mustache, and he spoke with a heavy British accent.

While Mandie and Celia were seated to the captain's left, Mrs. Taft and the senator sat on his right.

The girls groaned and whispered to each other when no one was looking, "Why do we have to sit right under his nose?" Mandie said between clenched teeth.

"And right in front of your grandmother and the senator," Celia muttered.

As the table filled, the girls found themselves the only young people there. Most of the other guests were even older than Mrs. Taft.

After everyone was seated, Captain Montrose turned to Mandie. "I'm very happy to welcome friends of President McKinley to my ship and my table," he said. "I've heard about your visit to the White House, Miss Amanda."

"You have?" Mandie questioned, folding and unfolding her hands under the table.

"Yes, you see it was in all the British newspapers— the story of how you have helped the Cherokee Indians," the captain explained. "I wish I could have met your other friends, too."

"Thank you, Captain Montrose," Mandie said. "But we didn't do anything special. You see, the gold belonged to the Cherokees in the first place. We just used it to build them a hospital."

"But without your leadership and knowledge the poor Indians would likely not have accomplished with it what you did," the captain added.

Mandie bristled. *Poor Indians!*

Celia touched Mandie's arm in a cautioning gesture.

Just then, from across the table, a man with wire-rimmed glasses spoke. "And have you heard anything from the President since your visit?" he asked.

Mandie recognized him as the man who had given Senator Morton the newspapers. Before the ship sailed, she had thought he was a visitor, not a passenger.

"No sir," Mandie replied. "Except for a note right after I got home. President McKinley is such a busy person. And his wife is so sickly, he has to take care of her, too."

"Do you expect to visit him again someday?" the man asked.

"Mister . . . uh . . . I don't believe I got your name, sir," Mandie stammered.

"I am sorry, Miss Shaw," the man apologized. "I thought perhaps you caught it when the captain introduced all of us. My name is Janus Holtzclaw. I believe we were both at the President's inaugural dinner in Washington."

"Oh yes, Mr. Holtzclaw." Mandie nodded. "President McKinley invited us to visit him again sometime, but there is nothing definite about that. Why do you ask all these questions?"

Mrs. Taft gasped, and others around the table cleared their throats.

Mandie didn't care what other people thought. She was determined to get to the bottom of this mystery. Why was this man so interested in her?

"I apologize again, my dear," Mr. Holtzclaw said, grinning. "I happen to own a newspaper, and I have a bad habit of asking too many questions, I suppose." He adjusted his wire-rimmed spectacles.

"I suppose I do, too, sir, and I apologize if I sounded rude," Mandie replied. She looked down at her plate, hoping to end the conversation. At least now she knew why the man gave the senator all those newspapers. He was in the business.

The captain picked up the conversation again. "We will be having a play in the music room after this meal is finished," he said. "If anyone would care to attend, I would be happy to escort you to the room."

Mandie shivered at the overly courteous way the captain spoke. There was something about that man. . . .

Immediately everyone at the table agreed to go to the play except Mandie and Celia. Mandie glanced at her grandmother for instructions, and Mrs. Taft told the girls they should come along with the senator and her to the play.

As everyone left the table, Mandie and her friend trailed along behind. Mandie turned to Celia and whispered, "I didn't see Charles anywhere." She looked around to be sure no one else could hear. "And I didn't see that strange woman, either."

"Charles probably eats with the help," Celia reminded her. "And maybe that woman eats at the second sitting."

"Let's go see if she's anywhere near our room," Mandie urged. Before Celia could reply, Mandie tapped Mrs. Taft on the shoulder, and she turned around. "Grandmother, Celia and I need to stop in our room for a second, we'll catch up."

"Well, all right," Mrs. Taft replied. "But make it fast, and be sure you find us. We'll save two seats next to us for the play."

The girls agreed and hurried down a cross hallway. As soon as they were out of sight of the adults, they lifted their long skirts and raced along the corridor to their room. There was no one in sight anywhere. Now and then they could hear someone talking in a cabin, but the corridor was deserted.

As they reached their door, Mandie sighed and opened it. "We didn't find her," she said, grabbing her kitten before he could get out. "Oh, Celia. I forgot about Snowball. He's got to have some supper."

"If we could find that Charles, maybe he would get some food for him," Celia suggested.

"But I'm not sure what he would think about Snowball," Mandie protested.

"Didn't your grandmother get permission for you to bring the kitten?" Celia asked.

Mandie rubbed Snowball's head. "I don't know," she replied. "I guess I assumed she did, but I'm afraid to take any chances."

Snowball looked as if he wanted her to pick him up, but she shook her head. "No, Snowball, you might snag your claws on all this lace and finery."

Suddenly Celia gasped, and Mandie looked up.

"Mandie, look! All the fruit is gone! Every single piece."

Mandie ran over to the table and picked up the empty bowl. "Well! I wonder who took it? And why!"

Just then there was a loud rap at the door, and when Mandie went to answer it, she was glad to see the steward's smiling face. He held a lovely vase of beautifully arranged fresh flowers.

"Excuse me, ladies," he said in his crisp British accent. "These were to be in your room before we sailed, but there was a mix-up of some sort. They're compliments of the captain."

Mandie hesitated a moment, then took the vase and set it down on the dressing table.

Charles talked with them for a few minutes, then started to leave.

"Wait," Mandie said. "I wonder if you would do me a big favor."

"Certainly, miss. Anything you desire," Charles said, half bowing.

"You see, I need some food—" Mandie stopped, not knowing how to explain the situation.

"For your kitten," Charles said with a smile. "I was just going to get him something after I delivered the flowers."

Mandie looked at him in surprise. "You knew about Snowball?"

"Of course, miss." He smiled. "You see, when I brought the bowl of fruit for you, I noticed him then. Poor kitten was lonely, being shut up in here." Charles stooped down and rubbed Snowball's soft fur as the kitten purred and rubbed against his legs.

"You don't mind if I keep him on the ship?" Mandie asked.

"No, I love animals, and so does the captain," Charles told her. "Now I'll get him supper if you'll excuse me."

"Wait." Celia stopped him. "You say you brought the bowl of fruit to us. But it's all disappeared." She pointed.

Charles stared at the empty bowl. "You ate it that fast?"

"We haven't touched it," Mandie said. "Why did you bring us so much fruit anyway?"

"That, too, is compliments of the captain," Charles explained. "I also left one in your grandmother's cabin next door, and the senator's across the way." He shielded his mouth as though divulging some great secret. "Confidentially, though, you two are the only ones to whom he sent flowers."

He grinned, then grew serious again. "I just cannot imagine who took all that fruit." He reached over and took the bowl. "Never mind," he said. "I'll just get you another one."

"Thanks so much," Mandie said as he started out the door. "Celia and I have to catch up with my grandmother now and see that play in the music room. Thanks."

Celia grabbed Mandie's arm. "Mandie!" she cried. "How do we find the music room? We don't even know where it is." She looked at Charles helplessly.

Before Mandie could reply, Charles offered to show them where it was. Shutting Snowball in their room, the girls followed the handsome steward down the corridor.

Mandie squeezed Celia's hand and whispered, "You said that on purpose, didn't you?"

Celia nodded and smiled as they caught up with the man.

"Do you have a crush on him?" Mandie teased after Charles left them at the music room. The play had not yet begun.

Celia raised her eyebrows, grinned, and silently led the way to the seats Mrs. Taft was holding for them.

Chapter 4 / Snowball Escapes

The sun shone brightly the next morning, and the ship's chaplain planned a Sunday church service in the open air on the main deck. Mrs. Taft insisted that the girls attend with her and the senator.

As the girls got ready, Mandie had a hard time waking up. "It doesn't seem like a vacation to me," she grumbled. "Having to get up so early is not fun after we had to stay up so late last night. That play was really silly, wasn't it?"

Celia let out a long sigh. "Cheer up, Mandie," she said, putting the finishing touches on her hair. "When we grow up, we can do whatever we please, and that includes sleeping late on vacation."

The connecting door opened and Mrs. Taft looked in. "Are you ready, girls?" she asked.

"Yes, ma'am," they said in unison. Picking up their bonnets, they quickly tied them on.

The deck chairs had all been placed in a large semi-circle, and the chaplain stood with his back to the rail. All of the crew that could be spared stood at attention in their bright uniforms around the rail.

Senator Morton led the way for Mrs. Taft and the girls,

and they sat near the edge of the chairs toward the front. The breeze wasn't as strong as it had been, and the ship seemed to float instead of bounce along as it had before.

The girls looked around, and Mandie whispered to Celia, "Not everyone is here. Some people got to sleep late."

"Maybe they're not Christians like us," Celia replied softly. "We're used to going to church on Sunday."

Mrs. Taft leaned forward and reached across the senator. "Girls!" she whispered, shaking her head.

Mandie and Celia straightened up immediately and listened as the chaplain delivered his sermon. As he talked about Jesus walking on the water, Mandie found that hard to believe after being on the ocean like this. Then she shook her head, irritated with her thoughts, and reminded herself that anything is possible with the Lord. *After all*, she thought, *He made the oceans and rivers and seas.*

Mandie let her gaze wander over the crowd in search of the strange woman as she listened to the chaplain. She was nowhere to be seen. But Charles stood in the middle of the lineup of the ship's crew, and Mandie noticed Celia glancing his way now and then.

After the closing "amen" of the service, Mrs. Taft rose quickly. "We'll go inside now, girls, and have some breakfast," she instructed. "After that you may bring your Bibles and books out here on the deck to read awhile if you like." She and the senator headed for the dining room. "I will be going to a meeting with other North Carolinians who are on board. We're making plans for our time in Europe. Come along, girls."

The girls followed. "Yes ma'am," they replied.

As they entered the dining room, the aroma made

Mandie glad they weren't sleeping through breakfast. As she and Celia moved through the buffet line, they filled their plates with sausage, bacon, eggs, hot biscuits, honey, jam, and "chips," which they learned was the British name for fried potatoes.

With plates piled high, the girls walked over to the small table where the senator and Mrs. Taft were already seated. "The only thing missing is grits," Mandie told her friend.

Celia giggled. "The British probably don't even know what they are," she said.

When they had finished their breakfast, Mrs. Taft and the senator excused themselves. "We're going to the tea room now for our meeting," Mrs. Taft told them. "Just be sure you two don't do anything you shouldn't."

"Of course not, Grandmother," Mandie assured her.

When the Senator and Mrs. Taft had left the room, the girls eagerly finished their food. "Let's hurry. I want to look around for that strange woman again," Mandie told her friend.

"Don't you think we'd better go back to our cabin and get our books and Bibles first?" Celia replied. "Remember what your grandmother said about reading."

"We'll get around to that," Mandie said. "I'd like to change my bonnet first. This one is too big and heavy."

"And we can look for that woman on our way to our room," Celia added.

As the girls headed in the direction of their cabin, they decided that most of the passengers must be lounging on the decks or in their rooms because there were very few people in the corridors. The girls watched for the strange woman, but she didn't cross their path.

Celia opened the door to their cabin and went in.

Mandie followed, leaving the door slightly ajar as she hurried to find a more comfortable bonnet in her hat box.

Celia almost tripped over a bowl on the floor next to the little table. A few tiny pieces of egg and bacon remained. "Looks like Charles has given Snowball his breakfast," she said.

Mandie glanced down at the bowl as she tied on another bonnet. "He did say he would look after her food. Let's go."

"Are we taking our Bibles and books now?" Celia asked.

Mandie started for the door. "Oh no! I left the door open!" she cried. "Where is Snowball? Here, kitty, kitty." She stooped to look under the few pieces of furniture he might have crawled under. "Celia! He's got out."

Celia ran to the door and looked down the corridor. "Mandie!" she exclaimed. "I see him way down yonder. Come on, hurry!"

The girls lifted their long skirts and raced down the corridor. Snowball stopped, looked back once, and quickly disappeared around a corner.

The girls ignored the people who stopped and stared as they raced after Snowball.

Mandie turned the corner. "He went this way," she called to Celia. Her friend followed. But when they got around the corner, Snowball was nowhere in sight.

Suddenly Celia pointed. "Look, Mandie!" she cried. "He's sitting on top of that laundry cart."

The girls hurried toward him. Snowball quickly jumped down and again disappeared around another corner. Every time the girls caught a glimpse of the white kitten, he immediately disappeared. They followed him down stairs and through opened doors, but he always managed to stay out of their reach.

Finally, after going down several flights of stairs, the girls came to an open door at the foot of the steps. They stopped to stare at what seemed like hundreds of people sitting around on a deck, talking loudly. Their clothes were ragged and threadbare. Dozens of children played in the crowded quarters, and a few people were eating from bags they held in their laps.

Mandie looked at Celia in confusion. "Who are these people?" she whispered loudly. "I haven't seen anyone like this anywhere we've been on this ship."

"I don't know," Celia answered in the same tone.

The people turned to stare at the two girls, and conversation instantly stopped. It was as though they were waiting to see what Mandie and Celia were up to.

Suddenly Mandie spotted Snowball. A little girl in an ill-fitting dress was holding him tightly and rubbing his head.

"Snowball!" Mandie cried. She sprang forward to take the kitten from the little girl.

"No, no!" the child cried. She jumped up and ran.

Mandie and Celia tried to follow through the crowd, but the people wouldn't move to let them through.

"That's my kitten that little girl has got!" Mandie shouted as she slipped between two husky men. Celia followed.

Still holding Snowball tightly, the child ran to a tall, thin woman and took refuge in her long, full skirt.

Mandie was almost out of breath as she came face to face with the woman. "Ma'am, that's my cat the little girl has," she said boldly.

The woman, who looked almost as young as Mandie,

bent down to speak to the child. "Violet, give the lady her kitten," she said firmly.

"Mine!" the child refused. "I found it."

The tall woman pushed back her bonnet, revealing blonde hair. She bent down beside the child and put her arms around her. "Now listen, Violet. It's the lady's kitten, not yours," she reprimanded. "Now give it to her at once."

The child twisted free and ran through the crowd.

The young woman stood. "I'm sorry," she said to Mandie. "Ever since our mother died, she tries to claim everything that comes across her path. I'll get the kitten for you."

Mandie's heart went out to the young woman. "Your mother died?"

"Yes, last week," she replied sadly. "My father thought it would be best if Violet and I went to stay with my mother's sister in England for a while. You see, my mother was English."

Mandie detected a slight British accent. "I'm sorry, Miss—"

"My name is Lily Masterson. Violet and I are sisters," the young woman explained. "She's only six years old. I was ten when she was born, and our mother had been sickly a lot, so I've always looked out for Violet."

Celia looked around the deck. "Where did all these people come from?" she asked.

Lily laughed. "Evidently, you belong in the first-class section," she replied. "This is what they call the steerage section. You see, if you don't have much money, you can ride here for a small fee. Only thing, there aren't any real rooms, and you have to sleep wherever you can find a place and eat whatever you can find. But sooner or later you'll get where you're going—same as all those first-class ladies and gentlemen.''

Mandie couldn't believe what she was hearing. "Lily, my name is Amanda Shaw," she said. "And this is my friend, Celia Hamilton. This is the first time either one of us has ever been on a ship. I thought everyone had accommodations like ours. I didn't even know there was such a place as this steerage section.''

She rubbed her brow thoughtfully. "Maybe you and your little sister could come up to our room and sleep. We only have two single bunks, but we could make pallets on the floor," she offered. "That would be better than this.''

"Oh no, no," Lily protested. "There are regulations on this ship. People in this section are strictly forbidden to go up to your section.''

Celia looked worried. "Do you not have a dining room to eat in?" she asked.

"For goodness sakes, no," Lily replied. "You bring your food with you when you get on the ship.''

"My goodness!" Mandie said in amazement. "I don't see how it could last all the way to England. Doesn't it spoil?''

The young woman smiled. "No, you have to bring things that won't spoil—like dried beef, hard bread, cheese and things like that," she explained. "Don't worry about us. We'll be all right. And once we get to England, our aunt has a nice house in the country and she has written and asked us to come.''

Violet peeked out from behind her sister's skirt. She was still holding onto Snowball. Lily quickly bent down, grabbed the kitten, and handed it to Mandie before the child knew what was happening.

"Mine!" Violet screamed, pulling at her sister's skirts.

Lily swung her sister up into her thin arms and hugged her tight. "Violet, that is that lady's kitten, not yours," she said firmly. "Maybe Aunt Emma will have a kitten and you can play with it."

The child leaned back to look into her sister's face. "Do you think she might?"

"I can't promise, but if she doesn't, maybe she'll allow us to get one for you," Lily tried to comfort her.

Violet pouted. "But she might not have one, and she might not get one for me," she said, glancing in Mandie's direction.

Mandie stepped forward and patted the child's blonde head. "I tell you what," she said. "If your sister will come to the hotel where we're going to be staying in London, I'll get you a kitten all your very own."

"We couldn't do that," Lily protested. "We're to stay overnight at a boardinghouse my aunt recommended in London and then we'll get the train the next morning. You see, the train goes right by my aunt's house in the country. My aunt knows the engineer, so he has promised to stop and let us off."

Celia's eyes grew wide. "That's great to have the train stop right at your door," she said.

Snowball was squirming to get down, and Mandie held him tighter. "You could still come by where we're staying," she offered.

"But where would you get a kitten in a country like that that you don't know anything about?" Lily asked.

"Oh, but my grandmother knows people all over Europe. I'm sure she could find a kitten for Violet," Mandie assured her.

Lily hugged her sister. "I think it would be better if you asked your grandmother about this first," she insisted.

"All right. I will then," Mandie promised. She started to leave, then turned back. "I'll come back soon and let you know what she says. Bye bye, Violet." She waved.

The child merely looked at her without a word. Lily set her sister down and waved to the girls as they headed for the stairs.

"I don't think I remember how far up we are," Celia said, "Do you?"

"You know I don't either," Mandie admitted as they started up, "but we'll find our way somehow." She scolded Snowball for squirming to get down. "And we're lost all because of you, Snowball."

Looking up, she stopped suddenly on the stairs. "Celia, I believe I saw that strange woman up there on the landing. Come on! Let's hurry."

They lifted their cumbersome skirts and hurried upward. At the landing they stopped to look around. There was no one in sight. Mandie turned to the right.

"Mandie, don't go wandering off," Celia warned. "I know for a fact that we came straight down at least three or four flights of stairs." She waited for her friend to return.

"You're right, Celia," Mandie agreed. She came back and started up the staircase again. "I guess we'd better try to find our way back instead of looking for that woman."

The girls took the stairs all the way up until they came to a set of heavy double doors. They stopped to rest.

"I think we came through these doors," Mandie said thoughtfully. Pushing one open, she peered around it, then quickly dashed through with Celia right behind her. "Come on. This is the way, and I just saw that woman again."

They barged ahead through doors, up more stairs,

and down corridors until they finally came to their section of the ship. But the strange woman had disappeared.

Mandie stopped to catch her breath. "Whew! That was a long trip!"

"It wasn't so bad going down, but having to come back up all those steps is too much," Celia agreed.

Mandie looked at the cabin numbers on the doors. "Now according to the numbers, we're on the right track," she said. "Hooray, we're right down this hallway!"

"And there comes your grandmother," Celia told her.

The girls hurried to meet Mrs. Taft at her door. Then going inside with her, they excitedly told her what they had discovered.

"Amanda, please pause to get your breath," Mrs. Taft scolded. "I can't understand a word you're saying." The older woman sat down.

Mandie and Celia sat on the bed, and Mandie let Snowball down as she explained where they had been. While she talked, Mrs. Taft listened with a surprised look on her face.

"So, you see Grandmother, you *can* find a kitten in London for the little girl, can't you?" Mandie asked. *"Please?"*

"Amanda." Mrs. Taft began. "You and Celia should never have intruded on those people down there. They are not allowed up here in our section, and you should respect their privacy too."

The girls looked at each other in stunned silence.

"But Grandmother, Lily was friendly with us," Mandie protested. "Besides, how could I have found Snowball if I didn't just keep following after him?"

"One of the stewards would have found him for you," Mrs. Taft replied. "You should be more careful and not let Snowball out of your room." She stood and took off her bonnet. "Now, I'm going to rest a few minutes. It will soon be time for the noon meal."

The girls stood and headed for their room.

"Grandmother, would you just give me permission to see those girls when we get to London so *I* can give Violet a kitten?" Mandie asked eagerly.

"Amanda, you know that's impossible," Mrs. Taft replied. "We're going to be staying at the Majestic Hotel, and who knows where they'll be staying?"

"Would you just give me permission to tell Lily where we're staying, so that *if* she can find it, she can come by?" Mandie persisted.

"Come by for what? We can't just sail into London and find a kitten just like that!" Grandmother snapped her fingers.

"If they came by, I could give them enough money to buy a kitten for Violet. Please?" Mandie pleaded.

"Amanda, you've got too soft a heart," Mrs. Taft told her. She paused. "I suppose I can give you permission for that much," she conceded. "But let me caution you. Don't go back down there to the steerage section. You send a note by the steward. Do you understand?"

Mandie impulsively hugged her grandmother. "Oh, thank you. Thank you, Grandmother."

Mrs. Taft hugged her granddaughter back. "Now leave me alone girls," she said. "I need to rest before we eat."

Mandie snatched up Snowball, and the girls went through the connecting door to their own room. As they sat down together on Celia's bunk, Mandie put Snowball down, and he played on the bed behind them. Mandie glanced over at the fruit bowl on the little table.

"Look, the bowl is full of fruit again!" she exclaimed. "Why don't we get the steward to take it to Lily and Violet with the note when we send it. I feel so sorry for those people having to travel like that."

"All right," Celia agreed. "That would be nice. Do you suppose we could find Charles and ask him to do all this for us?"

Mandie jumped up. "Let's see if he's at the end of the hallway." She caught hold of her kitten. "And, Mister Snowball, you don't get to go this time. You stay here." She set him down on the floor.

Carefully closing the door behind them, the girls went looking for Charles. To their surprise, they actually found him sitting on the stool at the little counter, doing some kind of paperwork. He looked up with a smile and greeted them.

Mandie leaned on the counter. "Charles, could we ask you to do us a favor, please?" she asked.

He stood up. "Why yes, ma'am. Anything you ask."

"You see, there's a place on this ship called the steerage section," Mandie began.

"Yes, I know, and you young ladies shouldn't never go down there," the steward warned. "There are some unsavory characters on that deck."

"That's why we want you to go for us," Mandie continued.

Charles looked shocked. "You want *me* to go to the steerage section? For what, miss?"

"There's a tall girl down there named Lily Masterson," Mandie explained. "She's about sixteen years old, and she has a little sister named Violet—"

"She's about six," Celia added.

"Right," Mandie said. "And I would like for you to take a note to them for me."

"Do you know these people, miss?" Charles asked.

"Yes we do," Mandie replied. "Would you do it for me?"

The steward hesitated. "If you say so, miss," he finally agreed. "But, mind you, I'm not positive I can find them. There must be hundreds of passengers down there."

"I'm sure you can find them," Mandie assured him. "Just ask someone where the girls are that had visitors from the first-class section this morning."

"You . . . went down there?" Charles was overwhelmed. "To the steerage?"

"Not on purpose," Celia quickly explained. "Snowball got lost, and when we chased him we ended up down there."

"And this little girl, Violet Masterson, had caught Snowball," Mandie added.

Charles shook his head. "Do you have the note ready?" he asked.

"If you'll just come to our room in a minute or two, I'll have it ready then," she assured him.

"Right-o," Charles replied, stacking his papers.

Back in their cabin, Mandie quickly found some stationery, wrote a brief note giving the name of their hotel in London, sealed it in an envelope, and wrote Lily's name on the outside.

When the steward knocked on the door a minute later, the girls asked him to also take their bowl of fruit to the Mastersons, but he protested.

"But we may never even eat it," Mandie argued. "We get so much to eat in the dining room."

"And those people don't have enough food," Celia added.

"All right," Charles gave in. "But I won't take your fruit.

I know where the fruit is kept, and I'll just get some for them."

"We won't tell anyone. Thanks a lot," Mandie said.

"It doesn't matter whether you tell anyone or not," Charles explained. "The fruit will be included in the price of your cabins. You may have as much as you wish, and I guess it doesn't matter if you wish to give some away."

"Great!" Mandie exclaimed. "Then will you take some down there to the girls every day?"

The steward hesitated.

"Please?" Celia begged.

Charles looked into her big brown eyes and smiled. "Anything you wish, miss. Now let me be off."

Mandie handed him the note. "Just in case you don't find the girls, would you please let me know?" she asked.

"Sure, miss. That I will do," he promised. "Cheerio!"

The girls frowned, puzzled.

"Cheerio?" Mandie questioned.

"Oh, sorry about that," he apologized. "You're Americans. Cheerio means goodbye in my country," he said on his way out.

The girls stood at the doorway and waved. "Cheerio!" they called as he vanished around a corner.

Just as Mandie was about to close the door, she spotted the strange woman going into a cabin down the corridor. She gasped. "There she is, Celia!" she whispered loudly.

Celia looked out. "Where?"

Snowball rubbed around Mandie's ankles, and she scooped him up. "She went into a room down there." She pointed.

"Now we know where she's staying, anyway," Celia said as Mandie closed the door.

"And we can watch out for her better because we know she's staying in this corridor," Mandie agreed.

Chapter 5 / Storm on the Ocean

In the middle of the night, a loud crack of thunder woke Mandie. She sat up in bed, her heart pounding. Outside the open porthole, lightning flashed again and again.

Mandie jumped down from her bunk, and Snowball followed. Mandie's legs felt rubbery as the ship lurched first to one side and then to the other. The ship's foghorn blew several times.

She bent down over the lower bunk. "Celia," she said, shaking her friend. "Wake up. There's a bad storm."

At that moment, the wind blew a chair across the cabin floor, and Mandie ran to shut the porthole. But the force of the wind was too strong.

"Celia!" she cried. "Come help me!"

Bleary-eyed, Celia stumbled over and helped Mandie get it closed. Then she slid down to the floor and sat there.

Mandie flipped the lamp switch, but the light didn't come on. "Oh, these newfangled lights!" she fussed. "No electricity! If this were a kerosene lamp, I could light it."

The connecting door opened, and Mrs. Taft stood

there holding a lighted oil lamp. She surveyed the room as the lamp cast weird shadows. "Amanda, Celia, are y'all all right?" she asked.

"Yes, Grandmother. We just got the porthole shut," Mandie replied. "Where did you get that lamp? All we have is this silly one that doesn't use kerosene."

"This was in my cabin," Mrs. Taft told her. "Don't you girls want to come in with me until the storm is over?"

"I'm all right," Mandie said. She glanced over at her friend, who was still sitting on the floor. "What about you, Celia?"

A loud crack of thunder sent Celia scrambling to Mandie's side. "I'll be all right," she said shakily. Turning to Mrs. Taft, she asked, "Do you think this ship is safe in such a bad storm?"

Mrs. Taft hesitated a moment before answering. "Why, Celia, I'm sure this ship has been through dozens of storms."

The ship swayed and Celia grabbed Mandie's hand. "But we're way out here in the middle of the ocean, and it's too far to swim to shore."

"Celia, we don't know how to swim anyway," Mandie said. "Grandmother, don't worry about us. We'll be all right. I'll sleep with Celia. I don't want to get thrown out of the top bunk when the ship sways."

"Well. . . . If y'all are sure you will be all right, I guess I will go back to bed," Mrs. Taft said, turning to leave. "I would leave this lamp, but I don't think we ought to leave it burning while we are asleep. It could fall off the table in all this pitching of the ship and set the place on fire. But if you need me, don't bother to knock, just come on in." She paused in the doorway. "Good night, girls."

"Good night, Mrs. Taft," Celia said. The ship lurched

again, and she gripped Mandie's hand tighter.

Mrs. Taft almost lost her footing.

"Good night, Grandmother," Mandie said. "Come on, Celia, let's get back in bed while we can see where we're going."

Her grandmother held the light high for them to see until they both got into Celia's bunk and pulled the sheet up over their heads. Then she went back to her room and closed the door.

"Celia," Mandie said in a quivering voice, "we ought to say our verse, don't you think?"

"You're right," Celia agreed. "Let's say it together."

Holding each other's hand, the girls quoted their favorite Bible verse, the one that always gave them confidence to get through problems. " 'What time I am afraid I will put my trust in Thee,' " they said in unison.

Mandie relaxed a little. "Now I feel better," she said. "God will take care of us."

"I know," Celia said. "He always takes care of us."

Feeling the warmth of God's care and the rocking of the ship, the girls soon drifted back to sleep.

When daylight came, they awakened to a hot, stuffy room with the porthole still closed. But when they looked out, they saw that it was still raining hard. The wind was blowing, but the thunder and lightning were gone.

"Celia," Mandie suggested, "do you think we could slip out on the deck for a little fresh air? It's hot in here, and if we open that porthole, everything will get blown around."

Celia hesitated a moment, then said, "Why not? We can just stay five minutes maybe and then come back."

Mandie walked over to the dressing table drawer and took out her watch. "My goodness," she said. "It's only

68

five minutes till six. I don't understand how we woke up so early after being up last night during that storm."

"The alarm clocks in our heads probably thought we were back home and had to get up for school." Celia laughed. "I sure hope we don't have any more storms like that one last night."

At that moment the ship lurched a little but nothing like it had the night before. Celia grabbed the post to her bunk bed.

Mandie laughed. "This ship is going to do that as long as the wind blows," she said. "Let's get dressed and go out before Grandmother wakes up."

As the ship continued to tilt from side to side, the girls managed to get dressed. Mandie carried Snowball with her and Celia led the way out into the corridor. They had to hold onto the handrail along the wall as they headed out to the deck.

When they pushed through the outside door, the wind blew their capes and their skirts. In an effort to hold her clothes down, Mandie released her kitten, but he seemed too frightened of the wind and rain to run off. He stayed close around her ankles.

Rain pelted their faces, and the wind was so strong that they could hardly walk. They hadn't gone more than a few feet when Celia stopped her friend. "Mandie, don't you think we ought to go back inside? This is terrible," she yelled above the roar of the wind and the waves beating against the ship.

Mandie shook her head. "Not yet," she yelled back, reaching up to hold the hood on her cape over her head.

Celia tried to keep her covered. "We should have worn bonnets," she hollered.

They stayed near the wall of the ship to shield themselves from the full force of the wind and rain, and slowly made their way down the deck. Finally Mandie paused to get her breath. Celia stopped by her side. The girls looked out over the lifeboats at the crashing waves below and shuddered.

Suddenly Mandie saw something move. She gasped. There was something or someone under the tarpaulin of one of the lifeboats.

"Celia, look at that lifeboat!" She pointed. "I think I saw something move in it."

Celia frowned. "I don't see anything, Mandie," she said. "It was probably the wind."

"The wind may have moved the tarpaulin, but I'm pretty sure I saw something under it," Mandie replied. "Come on. Let's go see." She led the way across the deck.

As the girls moved away from the protection of the cabin walls, the rain poured down on them. Without bonnets and with little protection from their capes, the girls were quickly drenched, but Mandie was determined to investigate.

Finally making it over to the lifeboat, Mandie grabbed the rail. "Celia!" she exclaimed. "There's somebody in that boat!"

Celia shrank back. "Mandie, let's go back inside."

But Mandie stepped over to the lifeboat and hung on. "Hey, you, inside that lifeboat," she yelled. "Come on out. We saw you."

At that moment the wind blew the tarpaulin back, uncovering a boy huddled in the bottom of the lifeboat. The girls stared at him in surprise. He was probably a little older than they were, dark, with black eyes and olive skin. As he stood up, they could tell he was stocky and a little taller than they were. For a moment he just stood there in the pouring rain, staring at them.

"What are you doing in that boat?" Mandie yelled above the roar of the wind.

The boy smiled but didn't reply. He just stood there, holding on to the ropes that were used to lower the lifeboat in case of emergency.

"Who are you?" Mandie hollered. "It's dangerous to be in a lifeboat in all this wind and rain. Don't you know that?"

Suddenly the boy yelled a torrent of foreign words, then just stood there smiling again.

Mandie and Celia looked at each other in confusion.

"What language is that, Mandie?" Celia asked.

"I don't know, but it isn't English," Mandie replied. She turned back to the boy. "Can you speak English?"

The boy shook his head and shrugged.

"I don't think he understood you," Celia remarked.

Again he spoke rapidly in a string of foreign words. Then he put his finger against his lips and crouched down in the boat.

"He wants us to understand that he's hiding!" Mandie exclaimed.

The boy stood up again and held his hand up to his opened mouth. Then he rubbed his belly.

"And he's hungry," Celia added.

"I wonder why he's—" Mandie stopped. Her eyes grew wide. "Oh no. He's a stowaway!"

Celia grabbed Mandie's arm. "Let's go," she urged.

Mandie shook her head. "He must be hiding from everyone because he isn't supposed to be on this ship." She yelled to the boy. "If you'll tell us why you're hiding, we'll get you something to eat."

The boy shook his head as though he didn't understand a word she said. Then he spoke again.

"Mandie!" Celia exclaimed. "I believe he's speaking French. They talk through their noses like that."

"I think you're right," Mandie said. "It does sound like that. I just wish I understood it." She paused. "Grandmother speaks French."

"Mandie, we can't let your grandmother know we've been out here," Celia reminded her.

"You're right," Mandie agreed. "What should we do? Should we bring him some food, or should we tell the captain about him?"

Celia shook her head. "Don't ask me for advice. Either way we'll get into trouble," she said. "We'd have to steal food from the dining room for him. And if we tell the captain everyone will know we were out here."

"But Celia, he must be hungry," Mandie protested. "I couldn't eat, knowing he's out here in that lifeboat starving to death." Mandie turned back to the boy and hollered, "We'll get you something to eat as soon as we can. It may be awhile, but we'll be back."

The boy smiled and disappeared again under the tarpaulin.

Suddenly aware of how drenched they were, Mandie picked up Snowball and started to run. "Let's hurry!" she called to Celia.

When they finally reached their cabin, they quickly pulled off their wet clothes and put on dry ones. Then they tried to dry their hair with towels.

"I'll never get all this hair put back up," Mandie complained. "I'm just going to braid it and leave it down." She began brushing out the tangles in her long damp hair.

"I guess I'll leave mine down, too, and tie it back with a ribbon," Celia decided. She rummaged in her trunk for a ribbon to match the dress she had put on.

Mandie looked down at her kitten, who was washing himself on the rug. She laughed. "At least Snowball is almost dry," she said.

Celia combed through her curly auburn hair. "Where are you going to get food to take to that boy, Mandie?" she asked.

Mandie began braiding her hair. "I'll have to figure out a way," she replied. "You know, Celia, I wonder why he's hiding on this ship, anyway. And if he's a foreigner, why is he sailing *away* from the United States? I wonder where he got on the ship?"

Celia tied the ribbon in her hair. "Well I'd like to know who he is," she said. "He's got to have a name."

"Do you suppose he's going to London like we are?" Mandie asked.

"I'm not sure this ship is going anyplace else," Celia replied.

At that moment, Mrs. Taft came through the connecting door. "Good morning, girls," she said cheerily.

"Good morning," the girls replied.

"I hope y'all were able to go back to sleep after that storm last night," Mrs. Taft said.

"We slept in Celia's bunk," Mandie told her.

"I don't believe we'll be able to go out on the deck today with all this rain and wind. Maybe we can find something to do after breakfast anyway," Mrs. Taft said. "I believe they are going to have a storyteller in the main salon after lunch, and there's music in the music room this morning."

The girls exchanged glances but said nothing.

"Shall we go to the dining room?" Mrs. Taft asked. She led the way out of the room.

As Mandie had hoped, Senator Morton was waiting for them in the corridor. With him around to entertain her grandmother it would be easier for Mandie and Celia to try to get some food to the stowaway somehow.

But Mrs. Taft and the senator stayed right with them the whole morning. After breakfast they walked down to the music room. A well-known opera singer gave a lengthy concert for the passengers, and then a group of actors put on an operetta.

Just when Mandie thought they might be able to get away from the adults, a tall woman stopped to talk to Mrs. Taft. "You all simply must come to the morning room," the woman said excitedly. "There's a magician performing there, and I understand he is really good."

"Thank you for telling us, Geneva," Mrs. Taft replied. "I am sure that will be a treat for the girls. We'll see you there."

Mandie and Celia looked at each other and rolled their eyes.

By the time the magician had finished his show, it was noon. The girls hadn't had much of a chance to talk all morning, and they couldn't discuss the boy in the lifeboat for fear the adults would hear them.

As they were finishing their noon meal, Mrs. Taft reminded them that the storyteller would be in the salon soon.

"Grandmother, would you mind if we went back to our room and rested awhile instead of going to hear the storyteller?" Mandie asked.

"I suppose this has been a busy day for y'all after that awful storm last night," Mrs. Taft said with a smile. "You're probably both tired."

Senator Morton suggested, "If the girls don't want to

74

listen to the storyteller, then you and I could go to the
lecture they're giving on France."

"Yes, we could," Mrs. Taft agreed. "You know girls
that we will be visiting France on this trip, too. But since
the lecture will be in French, I imagine it would be useless
for you, since you don't know the language yet." She
raised her eyebrows. "Which reminds me, Amanda, that's
one thing we need to see about. You will need some
French lessons."

Mandie's blue eyes twinkled as she thought of the boy
outside. "I'd love to learn the language, Grandmother."

"So would I," Celia added.

Mrs. Taft excused the girls from the table. "We will
see y'all at dinner tonight then," she said.

Mandie and Celia hurried back to their cabin as they
discussed the boy in the lifeboat.

"Have you figured out how we're going to get some
food for him?" Celia asked.

As they turned a corner in the corridor they spotted
Charles walking ahead of them.

"Yes I do know how!" Mandie said. "Let's catch up
with Charles."

Celia looked puzzled but followed her friend.

"Charles!" Mandie called as they neared the door of
their cabin.

The handsome steward turned around. "Yes, miss?
What may I do for you?"

"Uh . . . as a matter of fact, I'm hungry," Mandie replied
quickly. "Could you get some food brought to our room?"

Charles looked surprised. "Did you miss the noon
meal in the dining room?"

"Oh no," Mandie said, frantically trying to think of an
excuse. "But somehow I just didn't get enough to eat. We

were awake last night during the storm, and I guess it made us extra hungry. I could eat some more of that roast beef and those delicious salad greens," she said, ". . . and oh, another piece of that scrumptious coconut cake. And maybe a glass of milk to wash it down, if you don't mind."

Charles just stood there staring for a moment, then finally found his voice. "Yes, miss, of course," he said, "I'll get it for you right away." He started down the corridor, then turned back to Celia. "And did you want some food, too, miss?"

Celia smiled. "Oh no, thank you. I'm full."

Inside their cabin, Celia closed the door and looked at her friend. "Mandie, he's going to think there's something wrong with you, eating all that food when we've just come from the dining room!"

"So what? I had to think of something fast," Mandie said, flopping onto the settee. "And I needed to ask for a lot of food, because I don't know when I'll have a chance to get any more for that boy."

Charles soon returned with everything she had ordered and more—all neatly arranged in a straw picnic basket.

Mandie took the basket from him at the door, and smiled sweetly. "I really appreciate this, Charles."

Celia picked up Snowball so he wouldn't escape and stood behind Mandie at the door. "Did you find those people down in the steerage section and give them the note?" she asked the steward.

"Oh yes, miss," he replied. "The young woman seemed very grateful. But she did not send a reply."

"Thanks for everything, Charles," Mandie said, closing the door.

Even though the rain had almost stopped, the sky was still cloudy and the air was cool, so the girls bundled up for their jaunt on the deck. They tied scarves on their heads and put on their long, heavy cloaks. Mandie carried the basket under her cloak, but there was no one around when they reached the deck.

The boy must have been watching for them, because as they approached the lifeboat, he pushed back the tarpaulin and climbed down.

"Food," Mandie whispered loudly, pointing at the basket.

He smiled, accepted the food with a slight bow, then said something they couldn't understand. Before the girls could say anything more he had climbed into the lifeboat, waved, and disappeared under the tarpaulin.

Celia pulled her cloak tighter as the wind whipped around them. "That was quick," she said.

"Too quick," Mandie agreed. "I wanted to listen to him speak a little more to see if I could understand anything he was saying."

The girls turned to go back inside.

"No matter how long he talked Mandie, we couldn't have understood a word in that foreign language," Celia reminded her.

"The more I think about it, I'm certain he's speaking French," Mandie said. "I heard Grandmother speaking it to the French maids at the White House."

Mandie quickly opened the door to the corridor, and the girls almost collided with the strange woman. They stood gaping as the woman rushed past them and disappeared outside on the deck.

"Let's follow her!" Mandie suggested.

"No, Mandie," Celia protested, "We aren't supposed

to be outside, remember? We told your grandmother we would be in our room resting."

"I guess you're right," Mandie said, in disappointment. "We'd better get back to our cabin. But sooner or later I'm going to find out who that woman is and why she always seems to be spying on us."

"What makes you think she was spying on us just now?" Celia asked, as they hurred down the corridor.

"Well, she must have been standing right inside the door looking out when we came in," Mandie replied. "We almost knocked her over! Just give me time. I'll get to the bottom of it."

Chapter 6 / The Newspaper Story

During the next several days the girls had Charles bring food to their cabin once a day. He occasionally remarked about how surprised he was that two young girls could eat so much. But as soon as he left each time, Mandie began planning how to get the food to the boy in the lifeboat without being seen.

Then one day they were almost caught. It was in the middle of the afternoon. Mrs. Taft and the senator had gone to a lecture. Clouds covered the sky and strong winds rocked the ship.

Mandie checked the basket of food Charles had just brought. "Don't you think we could just run out there and back without being seen right now?" she asked Celia.

Celia sat on the settee, playing with Snowball. "I wouldn't be able to say, Mandie," she replied. "This whole episode has me worried. We could really get into trouble with your grandmother, and also with the captain."

Mandie sat down beside her and put the basket on the floor. "Celia, I don't think Charles would go tell the captain about the food, would he?" she said thoughtfully. "Besides, I think Charles actually believes we eat the food."

"You're forgetting something, Mandie," Celia re-minded her. "Do you remember hearing Charles say we could have all the fruit we want because it is all charged to this cabin? So someone is keeping a record of every-thing for each cabin."

Mandie gasped and said, "Oh, my goodness, I had forgotten he said that. Maybe I could let Charles in on our secret so he wouldn't tell about the food."

"But he owes his loyalty to the captain, not to us. Therefore, he'd probably go straight to Captain Mon-trose," Celia replied, as Snowball jumped down to the floor.

Mandie sighed and exclaimed, "Oh, well, I'll just keep on giving that boy food until someone does catch up with me. I can't let him starve to death."

But that very day something happened. The girls had looked outside through the glass in the door as they always did before going out on the deck, but they had not seen anyone. Mandie, who always carried the basket under her heavy cloak, pushed open the door and led the way toward the lifeboat. About halfway there the handle on the basket suddenly came off and the basket crashed to the floor, scattering food everywhere.

Mandie quickly stooped down to pick it all up with Celia's help.

"Oh, Celia, I've got to get this cleaned up," Mandie exclaimed.

As she reached for a boiled egg that had survived the splatter, a dark skirt moved in front of her. She looked up to see the strange woman walking past them. But she suddenly stopped to view the mess.

"I . . . I . . . just spilled my lunch," Mandie mumbled, hurriedly picking up the last of the mess.

The woman didn't say a word but walked on down the deck.

Celia remarked, "She's headed toward the front of the ship."

"You mean the bow, Celia," Mandie reminded her. "Remember our lessons about ship language? Now we're going to the stern, which is the rear, to go back inside." She glanced around quickly to be sure she had gotten everything.

"Are we not taking the food on to that boy?" Celia asked.

Mandie paused. "Well, I didn't know whether he'd want it after it's been on the floor. But this is all we can get for him today, so I guess I'll just go on and give it to him."

"Some of it was wrapped and wasn't damaged," Celia said. "He can give the squashed stuff to the fish."

As they returned in the direction of the lifeboat, Mandie kept a watch out again for the strange woman in black. "I just can't figure out what that woman is up to," she said. "She's always hurrying here and there. She did see all that food, and she may just tell my grandmother, if she knows who she is."

"And if she does that, you can guess what will happen next." Celia looked worried.

Mandie shrugged.

When they reached the lifeboat, the boy came out from under the tarpaulin as usual, and climbed down to take the basket from the girls.

Mandie turned to Celia. "I wish I knew how to speak his language so I could tell him what happened to the food," she said. Looking at the boy, she raised the cloth a bit and pointed to the basket handle. "Sorry, but I dropped it. See the handle fell off,' " she tried to explain with motions.

The boy just smiled, took the food, and jumped back into the lifeboat as he always did. He pulled the tarpaulin over and was out of sight.

The girls hurried back toward their room. "He could surely see the condition the food was in, but I suppose he was hungry enough to eat it anyway." Mandie made a face.

Once inside the cabin they spotted a handwritten note propped on the dressing table and rushed over to see what it said.

Mandie began to read, "Amanda and Celia, Mrs. Taft and I were given some delicious sweets at a meeting we attended this afternoon. I saved mine for you girls. You may go into my room and get it. I didn't think it was safe from Snowball in your cabin."

"Senator Morton thought of us. How nice!" She smiled.

"Let's get it now," Celia suggested. "I feel like something sweet."

They knocked on the senator's door to be sure he wasn't in his room, then slowly opened it and peeked inside.

"That must be it on the dressing table." Mandie pointed, crossing the room. A dainty little handmade paper basket was filled with bonbons. "Here, Celia, have some. I'll eat mine later."

As she turned around, her eye caught sight of the newspapers on the table nearby. "These must be the papers Mr. Holtzclaw gave the senator before we sailed," she said. She eagerly paged through them, fascinated as she was with news accounts.

Suddenly a headline caught Mandie's attention. She held it up to get a closer look, and gasped. "Celia, look at this!" she cried, pointing to a photo of a young boy. "Who *is* that?" Her hands were shaking.

Celia put down the candy. "Oh no!" she exclaimed, hovering over Mandie's shoulder to read the article.

"The stowaway is Jonathan Lindall Guyer, the third. His father is one of the richest men in America!" Mandie could hardly get the words out. She was out of breath.

"And look there," Celia pointed. "It says he is believed to have been kidnapped, and his father is offering a huge reward."

"He's an only son and heir," Mandie read on. "His mother died when he was two months old."

Celia grabbed Mandie by the shoulder and turned her around. "Do you know what else this means?" she asked.

Mandie read her mind. "He speaks English!" she almost shouted. "What a conniving—Wait till I see him again. Will I have some things to say!"

Celia shook her head in disgust. "We ought to just turn him in and collect that reward."

"What a good idea!" Mandie said. Carelessly folding the newspaper, she tucked it under her arm. "Come on, let's show him this paper right now. We can return it later."

"Let's shed these cloaks first, Mandie. I'm terribly hot," Celia said, slipping out of hers.

"Bring the candy," Mandie reminded her. "We can leave it in our room."

Hurrying back into their cabin, the girls hung up their cloaks and put the candy on the dressing table. Just then Mrs. Taft opened the connecting door. Something had obviously upset her.

"Amanda, what were you and Celia doing out on the

deck with a basketful of food?" She looked very distraught.

Mandie blushed, and stammered, "You see ... we, uh— Grandmother, it was a picnic basket—"

"A picnic basket!" she exclaimed. "Where on earth did you get a picnic basket? Surely you weren't planning to have a picnic on the deck!"

"Well, yes, and uh—The handle broke, and the food spilled everywhere," Mandie explained.

"It won't happen again, Mrs. Taft," Celia added, trying to help Mandie.

"It certainly will not happen again!" Mrs. Taft almost shouted.

Celia cringed. She had never seen Mrs. Taft so angry.

The woman folded her arms and shook her head. "Such disgraceful conduct for two young ladies. And especially from such good families!"

"I'm really sorry, Grandmother," Mandie apologized.

"Where did you get the food?" she questioned further. "You ate your noon meal in the dining room. Do you mean to tell me you were going to eat again before dinner?"

The girls both looked down at the floor, afraid to tell Mrs. Taft the truth.

Snowball rubbed around Mandie's ankles and she picked him up. "I know we ate, but—"

Before she could explain, Mrs. Taft interrupted, "If I hear of any more such conduct unbecoming to young ladies, we will get the next ship home as soon as we reach London. If you cannot conduct yourselves in a proper manner, you will have to return to your school and learn some things about deportment."

"Yes, ma'am. I'm terribly sorry," Mandie replied

meekly. She smoothed Snowball's fur and cuddled him close.

Not able to look into the woman's face, Celia spoke up, "Mrs. Taft, I—I owe you an apology, too. My mother did put me in your care, and I am truly sorry I have disappointed you."

Mrs. Taft sighed deeply and turned to leave. "Both of you will stay here in your room until dinner. I will come for you when it's time." She entered her cabin and closed the connecting door.

The girls both plopped down on the settee, and looked at each other wide-eyed.

"Whew! Was Grandmother upset! I'm sorry, Celia. I should have told her the whole thing was all my fault so she wouldn't blame you, too," Mandie said.

"It wasn't all your fault!" Celia countered. "I've been right with you in everything. And I didn't have to be."

"But I started it," Mandie insisted. "And to think we've been fooled by that lying Jonathan Lindall Guyer, the third. I can't wait to get my hands on him."

"Right," Celia agreed. "He's going to be sorry."

Mandie retrieved the newspaper from the dressing table. Spreading it on the floor, she sat down on the rug to look at it again. Celia joined her.

Mandie slapped her hand down on the newspaper photo, and shook her head. "I can hardly stand to look at that boy's face," she said.

"What are you going to do now?" Celia asked.

"I'm still going to confront him with this newspaper just as soon as I get the chance," Mandie said with determination.

"Have you guessed how your grandmother found out about the food basket?" Celia asked.

Mandie gasped. "That strange woman must have told her," she said. "You know, I didn't even think about how she'd found out. I was so shocked I couldn't think about it."

"It must have been that woman all right," Celia agreed. "I don't remember seeing anyone else around."

Mandie pounded her fist on the floor. "I want to know who that woman is!"

Celia shrugged. "Well, I don't know how we're going to find out."

"I wonder how she knew who my grandmother was," Mandie pondered. "I think I'll just ask Grandmother if she knows her."

Snowball walked across the newspaper and curled up by Celia. She smiled and petted the kitten. "Don't you think we ought to let things calm down and not bring up the subject again for a while?"

"I'd rather get it all straightened out once and for all," Mandie said. "I'll just ask Grandmother as soon as I get a chance."

The girls spent the rest of the afternoon doing nothing in particular, so they were glad when it was time to start getting dressed for dinner. Mandie chose one of her prettiest dresses—a blue silk, gathered at the waist, with a deep flounce around the hem. Since they were in no hurry, she took the time to pile her hair high on her head, leaving some long curls around her face.

Before the mirror, Celia put her hands on her hips. "You look simply gorgeous, Mandie!" she said with a hint of envy. "My naturally curly hair is naturally unmanageable in damp weather." She tried to tie it up with a pink ribbon to match her dress, but it simply would not stay in place.

"Let me fix it for you," Mandie offered. Picking up Celia's brush, she went to work on the thick auburn curls. By the time she had finished, she felt a professional hairdresser couldn't have done better.

Celia smiled at her reflection in the mirror. "Oh, Mandie, thank you!" she exclaimed. "I think perhaps I look gorgeous, too," she giggled.

Mandie laughed, too. "With all these *gorgeous* clothes we got for this journey we shouldn't have any trouble looking gorgeous all the time!"

Just then the connecting door opened, and Mrs. Taft came into the room. "I see you girls are ready," she said simply. It was difficult for Mandie to tell whether or not her grandmother was still angry. Mrs. Taft looked lovely herself, adorned in ruffles and lace from head to toe. "I believe the senator is waiting," she told them. "Let's be on our way."

When they met Senator Morton in the corridor, he smiled broadly and exclaimed, "My! Three beautiful women to escort in one night! What have I done to deserve this?" He winked at the girls, and Mandie guessed that he knew of the incident with the food basket, and was trying to cheer them.

Seated at the captain's table again for dinner, Mandie began to feel uneasy about the direction in which the conversation was shifting.

After complimenting the girls on their appearance, Captain Montrose added, "I do hope the food on this ship is not too rich. I'd hate to see such beautiful ladies become plump."

Celia squeezed Mandie's hand under the table. Did the captain know that Charles had been bringing food to their room? What caused him to make such a remark?

Mrs. Taft laughed heartily. She leaned over to Mandie and Celia. "You see, dears, I told the captain just this afternoon that I do believe I am gaining a little weight from all the good food on his ship."

Everyone laughed, and Mandie felt relieved.

After dinner, Mrs. Taft suggested that she and the senator and the girls all go for a promenade on the deck to aid digestion and burn up some of the extra calories.

By then it was dark, and as they strolled around the deck, Senator Morton and Mandie's grandmother stopped by the railing to gaze at the stars and the calm ocean below.

Suddenly Mandie realized how very close they were to the lifeboat where Jonathan was hiding. She was afraid to speak, knowing how easily a person's voice carried in the stillness of the night. Jonathan might think she and Celia had come to see him, and climb out of the boat.

Senator Morton spoke first. "There's going to be an old-fashioned gospel singing in the music room in a few minutes. Would you young ladies like to join us?"

"Oh yes, thank you." Mandie was relieved. "We'd love to go, wouldn't we, Celia?"

Celia looked puzzled but nodded.

The gospel singing turned out to be one of the most interesting events the girls had attended on the ship. Mandie loved to sing. She'd always said the best part of church was to lift your voice in praise to your Maker.

Mrs. Taft leaned forward and whispered to the girls, "This reminds me of the Quaker meetings I attended when I was young. Only we sang anything we wanted to— everyone all at once! It's all so invigorating and inspiring!"

"I love it, too," Mandie agreed.

"I didn't do too well," Celia said when they'd finished.

"I kept hearing the words from the other side." She laughed and they all laughed with her.

No further mention was made of the food, and after the gospel singing Mandie felt the tension had been broken. But as her grandmother said good night in the hall, Mandie asked if she could talk to her alone. "I just want to ask you a question," she said. Celia went on to their room.

"Of course, dear," Mrs. Taft replied as the senator bade them good night. "Come on in."

Inside, Mandie didn't sit down, but got right to the point. "Grandmother, who is the woman who told you about the picnic basket?" she asked.

Mrs. Taft looked puzzled. "I don't know who told me about it. I found a note stuck in my door. Here, I'll show it to you," she said. Walking over to the dressing table, she opened the drawer, took out a small piece of paper, and handed it to Mandie.

Mandie scanned the note quickly.

It read:

Mrs. Taft, I'm sure you will want to know that your grand-daughter and her friend spilled a whole basket of food all over the deck today. Very unladylike, don't you agree?

A concerned friend.

Mandie took a deep breath and handed the paper back to her grandmother.

Mrs. Taft placed it back in the drawer. "That's all I know, dear," she said.

Mandie sighed. "I know it must have been that strange woman who follows Celia and me around all the time," she said in exasperation. "We see her on the deck and in the halls, but we have never seen her in the dining room or at any of the events we've attended."

Mrs. Taft's brow wrinkled in concern. "A strange woman follows you around?" she said in disbelief. "Why, Amanda? What does she look like? Do I know her?"

"I don't know. She has a cabin right down this corridor somewhere," Mandie tried to explain. "I'm not sure exactly which one, but one night we saw her enter one of them. We were too far away to tell which."

"What does she look like?" Mrs. Taft asked.

"She's not very tall," Mandie replied. "Stoop-shouldered and thin. She has gray hair and black eyes and a real sharp chin. Her clothes look expensive, but she always wears black. And, oh, she has some flashy diamonds on her fingers, and she usually wears a huge brooch at her neck."

Mrs. Taft listened carefully, still puzzled. "How old would you say she is?"

"A lot older than you, Grandmother," Mandie said.

"Does she sound southern?"

"We've never even heard her speak, but to look at her, I'd say she's definitely not a southerner."

"How can you tell without hearing her accent?"

"She doesn't *look* like anyone I've ever known," Mandie explained.

"I'm sorry, dear, but I just don't know who this woman could be," Mrs. Taft said. "Let's sleep on it and maybe in the morning my memory will be better."

Mandie turned to go, then suddenly threw her arms around her grandmother. "Good night," she said softly. "I love you. A whole lot." Then she kissed her on the cheek.

Mrs. Taft held her granddaughter tightly. "I love you, too, Amanda. More than I could ever say. Even when you exasperate me, I still love you. You know that, don't you, dear?"

"Oh yes, Grandmother," Mandie said. "I'm sorry I always seem to get into such strange predicaments."

Grandmother gave her a kiss on the cheek and they said good night again.

When Mandie closed the connecting door, she saw that Celia was already in her bunk. As she readied herself for bed, she told her about the conversation with her grandmother. "Guess what, Celia?" she said. "That strange woman did not *tell* my grandmother about the food basket. She left a note in her door. At least, I assume the woman wrote it, but Grandmother doesn't think she knows her."

Celia sat up in her bed. "That *is* strange," she said, wrinkling her nose.

Dressed in her nightgown, Mandie stood in front of the mirror and began taking her hair down. "I've been thinking about that boy—Jonathan," she said. "Why don't we get up early and go out there and confront him before anyone else is up?"

"All right," Celia agreed.

"Maybe that strange woman won't be up yet either," Mandie said. Turning off the light, she put Snowball up on the top bunk and climbed up herself. Snowball walked around stretching his legs, finally curling up at her feet.

The girls lay awake for some time discussing what they would say to Jonathan Lindall Guyer, the third, in the morning.

Chapter 7 / Reward Money?

Mandie awoke as soon as the first rays of sun crept over the waters of the Atlantic Ocean. Climbing down from the upper bunk, Snowball tumbled behind her and fell onto Celia's bunk.

Celia gasped with fright, and Snowball leaped to the floor.

"Sh-h-h!" Mandie whispered to Celia. "It was just the cat! We don't want to wake Grandmother."

"You're right," Celia whispered back.

The girls dressed quickly, and Mandie eased the door open to see if anyone was in the passageway. "Come on," she said softly, "It's clear. Be sure Snowball doesn't get out."

Celia followed her into the hallway, giving Snowball a nudge, and closing the door behind her.

Once on the deck, they found a crewman working on something near the door, but the girls ignored him and went on their way.

Jonathan did not step out as they approached his lifeboat, like he usually did.

"He's probably still asleep," Mandie told Celia. She

softly called, "Hey, are you in the boat?"

The boy threw back the tarpaulin in one stroke and rubbed his eyes. Yawning, he climbed out, and jumped down in front of them.

Mandie began to feel her anger rise. She hardly knew where to begin, so she said his name. "Jonathan Lindall Guyer, the third! You must think we are a couple of pretty simple girls to have fallen for your act—pretending you didn't understand English."

The boy's face turned red. "I am truly sorry," he said. "I—I was afraid when you found me. I couldn't think what to say, so it seemed the easiest to just pretend not to understand what you were saying." He shrugged sheepishly. "I am very fluent in French, so I just spoke it instead. How did you ever find out who I am?"

Mandie reached inside her cloak and pulled out the newspaper with his picture in it.

Jonathan's mouth dropped open. He tried to grab the paper, but Mandie didn't trust him. She secured it firmly, afraid he would destroy it or refuse to give it back.

"You can't have this paper, because it doesn't even belong to me," she told him. He silently read the article while she held the paper.

When he looked up he asked, "Where did you get this newspaper?"

"The owner of the newspaper firm brought it on board before we left Charleston," Celia told him.

Mandie quickly folded the paper and set her gaze on the boy. "Well, what do you have to say for yourself?"

Jonathan shifted from one foot to the other. "I really don't know what to say," he answered. "If I told you the truth, you would never believe me."

Mandie frowned. "*Try* us!"

Jonathan walked in a circle, rubbing his chin. Then he looked straight at the girls. "All right, believe it or not, I am trying to get to Paris," he began. "I have an aunt and uncle there who are newspaper people, and I want to live with them."

"Why didn't you just tell your father that?" Mandie asked. "He must be worried to death, thinking you've been kidnapped."

"I didn't tell him for the simple reason that he would not have allowed me to go." Jonathan swallowed hard. "He keeps sending me off to expensive private boarding schools, and I'm tired of it. I want to live like a normal boy and have normal, everyday friends."

He shifted his weight again. "The boys at school are snobs. All they think about is who has the richest father, and who spends the most money on clothes. None of them will have to work for a living, so they don't even try to learn anything. School's a joke for them," he said solemnly.

"Why couldn't you stay at home and go to a school near where you live?" Celia asked.

"Because my father is hardly ever at home," Jonathan explained with a sigh. "He goes all over the world on business, and he thinks if he sticks me in these private schools he won't have to worry about me."

"What about your mother?" Mandie asked.

Jonathan's face clouded. "I don't have a mother," he said. "She died when I was a baby. Didn't you read that in the paper?"

"Yes. I'm sorry, I forgot," Mandie apologized. "And I'm sorry your mother died. But Jonathan, you're all your father has, and you ought to think about how he must feel, not knowing whether or not he'll ever see you again.

I know from sad experience that it doesn't pay to run away from home. I've done that myself. Why wouldn't your father let you visit your aunt and uncle?"

"I just know he wouldn't," Jonathan said firmly. "My aunt and uncle both work, and I'd be home alone when I'm not in school, except for the housekeeper. My aunt is my mother's sister, and I have never even met her and her husband. But she has always written to me saying that they would like to have me come and visit them. So that's why I am going to Paris."

"I wouldn't be too sure about that," Mandie told him. "My grandmother knows about the extra food we have been getting for you. She doesn't know what we have been doing with it, but she knows we had it out here on the deck. We won't be able to bring you any more. And I think we have to tell the captain about you."

"Oh no, please—please," Jonathan begged. "Don't tell the captain I'm here. He would lock me up somewhere on ship and put me off at the next port. From there, the police would take charge. Please don't put me through that."

"But it would be for your own good," Mandie said. "The police would send you back to your father, and he would be relieved to have you home, I'm sure."

"He must love you," Celia reminded him. "Look at the big reward he's offering."

Jonathan had an idea. "I'll tell you what! If you girls keep quiet, I'll see that you get that reward," he promised. "And when I get to Paris, I'll have my aunt let my father know where I am. Please?"

"But we don't even need the money," Mandie protested.

Jonathan's eyes widened. "You mean you would refuse all that cash? Just think what you could do with it."

"Money isn't everything, you know, Jonathan," Mandie replied. "You're just like the other boys at your school. Money, money, money—that's all some people think about." She shook her head. "Celia and I have already deceived my grandmother about the reason for the extra food, and I don't want to add any more problems."

"But you don't have to *do* anything," Jonathan assured her. "What I want is for you to do nothing. Just pretend you never saw me. Will you?"

"How are you going to get anything to eat if we don't bring it?" Mandie asked.

"Look here, Miss—What is your name, anyway?" Jonathan asked.

"Amanda Elizabeth Shaw, Mandie for short, and I'm from Franklin, North Carolina," Mandie introduced herself. "And this is my friend, Celia Hamilton, from Richmond, Virginia. We're traveling with my grandmother, Mrs. Norman Taft."

The boy's dark eyes grew wide in shock. "Mrs. Norman Taft?" he repeated.

Mandie frowned. "Yes, why? Do you know her?"

A curious look came over Jonathan's face. He cleared his throat, then hesitated a moment as though carefully considering his reply. "Mrs. Norman Taft is your grandmother?"

"I said yes," Mandie answered impatiently. "And I asked if you know her."

"No, I don't *know* her," Jonathan replied. "But I know who she is. Are you aware that Mrs. Norman Taft owns the ship we're sailing on?"

Mandie and Celia stared at each other a moment in silence.

"*My* grandmother owns this ship?" Mandie repeated slowly, incredulously.

"You must be mistaken," Celia added.

"I'm sorry, but I'm not mistaken," he insisted. "My father tried to buy the ship line from her this past winter, and she wouldn't sell. The company is British based, but she owns it—lock, stock, and barrel."

"Ship *line*? I thought you said she owned this ship." Mandie was confused.

"She owns the ship and the whole shipping company," Jonathan explained.

Mandie looked at Celia. Celia shrugged. "Well, you know your grandfather was very wealthy, Mandie. And I suppose he left everything to your grandmother."

"But why wouldn't she tell me she owned the ship?"

"You explained before," Jonathan volunteered. "Money isn't everything. She probably wants to be treated like everybody else."

"Just wait till I see my grandmother!"

"Calm down, Mandie!" Celia fussed. "We can't let her know that we know. She would want to know how we found out!"

"Oh, you're right," Mandie moaned. She thought for a moment. "To get back to your problem, Jonathan, we can't keep bringing food to you. If we got caught, well . . . You just don't know my grandmother. She said if we got into trouble again, we'd get the next ship home as soon as we arrive in London!"

"Look," Jonathan said. "I know if you're Mrs. Norman Taft's granddaughter, you really don't need the reward money, but isn't there something special you could do with that much money all your own?" He watched closely for Mandie's reaction.

Mandie thought about it. "No," she said slowly. "I couldn't deceive my grandmother again."

"I'm not asking you to deceive her," he said again. "Just forget about me. I can take care of myself."

Celia nudged Mandie. "Say, what about the Cherokee school? We could use the money for that. Of course, that is if we don't have to do anything dishonest to get it."

"Cherokee school?" Jonathan perked up. "You mean Indians? A school for Indians?"

"Yes," Celia said proudly. "Mandie is one-fourth Cherokee, and we're going to help build a school for them. She has already built a hospital for them."

Jonathan smiled at Mandie. "What a great thing to do with the money! In fact, if you'll agree not to turn me in, I'll add a few thousand dollars of my own money to it for the Indians."

"Two against one," Mandie grumbled. "All right. I won't tell anyone about you, but you'll have to fend for yourself from now on."

"Thank you, thank you," Jonathan said, smiling at Mandie. "I'll take care of myself. Don't worry. And I'll make arrangements for the money when we get off the ship. Where will you be staying?"

"The Majestic Hotel in London, but I don't know where else," Mandie replied. "We're also going to Paris."

"Now that everything is settled, we'd better get back to our cabin before we get in trouble," Celia reminded her.

"Right. Goodbye, Jonathan," Mandie said, and quickly walked with Celia toward the door to the corridor.

———

The next day, when they'd returned from breakfast,

Mandie noticed that the bonbons the senator had given them were missing.

Mandie looked at the table where they had been. "Did you eat all the candy?" she asked Celia.

Celia looked around. "No, I haven't even touched it since we put it there."

"I wonder what happened to it then?"

"Maybe Charles ate it," Celia said with a giggle.

"Oh, no, not proper Charles," Mandie reasoned. "He's not the kind to go around eating girl's candy."

"Maybe that strange woman came in here and took it," Celia suggested.

"I doubt it," Mandie said. "It's just a puzzle." She sighed. "Oh, well, it doesn't really matter to me."

"Or me," Celia added.

But when the girls returned to their room after the noon meal, they found all the fruit missing.

"Hey!" Mandie cried. "Now all the fruit is gone."

Celia let out a big sigh. "I just don't understand what's going on, Mandie," she said.

Mandie shook her head slowly. "I did tell Charles to take our fruit to those people in the steerage section, but he said he'd get some from storage for them, not take it from our room. Remember? You don't think he decided to take ours today, do you?"

"We could ask him," Celia replied.

But when they asked Charles about it later that day, he said he didn't have any idea what had happened to the fruit in their room. He was taking fruit from storage each day for Lily and Violet. Apologizing for the incident, he offered to get Mandie and Celia more fruit for their room.

"Thanks, Charles," Mandie said. "And if you ever happen to see anyone going into our room, would you please let us know right away?"

"Of course, miss," he promised. "But I'm not always around here because I take care of other passengers around the corner."

When the girls returned to their cabin to dress for the evening meal, they found their fruit bowl was full again. Just as Mandie was about to close the door, she spotted the strange woman hurrying down the corridor. "There's that woman!" she cried. "Let's see where she goes."

Before Celia could protest, Mandie was out the door and racing down the passageway. The woman turned the corner and disappeared, and Celia soon caught up with Mandie.

She was examining a piece of paper she had just picked up from the floor. "What is this?" she wondered aloud. "It says, 'Majestic Hotel,' that's all."

"Did that woman drop it?" Celia asked.

"I'm not sure, but I think she did," Mandie said. "She must have seen me following her because she turned around the next corner down there, and I think she went into a cabin."

"We'd better get dressed, Mandie," Celia reminded her, "or we'll be late for dinner."

"You're right." Mandie followed Celia back to their room. "You know, this paper looks dirty," she said as they stopped outside their cabin.

"Yeah. Like it's been walked on a few times," Celia guessed.

"Well, I didn't step on it, and I didn't see anyone else in the hallway," Mandie said.

Inside their room, Snowball came up to meet them. Mandie picked him up and dropped the piece of paper in their dressing table drawer. "All right, Snowball," she said. "I'll pet you now, but after I get into that fancy gown I won't be able to hold you."

Celia glanced through the dresses hanging in her closet. "It's the same old story," she said. "What shall I wear to dinner?"

"I'm getting tired of all this dressing up, too," Mandie agreed. "And all the food—I think we eat too much, especially when I think that Jonathan is probably not getting anything since we stopped taking food to him."

"I don't think he'll starve to death," Celia said with a twinkle in her big brown eyes. "He's too smart for that. He'll find something to eat somewhere."

Chapter 8 / Unwanted Visitor

After breakfast the next morning, Mandie and Celia went for a stroll on the deck to talk.

"You know, Celia," Mandie said, "this has been a mysterious voyage—finding a stowaway on board, a strange woman following us around, discovering the steerage section, not to mention the disappearing candy and fruit."

They paused a moment near the opened porthole of their cabin. "And don't forget that piece of paper with the words 'Majestic Hotel' written on it," Celia reminded her. "I sure hope everything gets solved so we can enjoy our stay in Europe."

"I wonder what London will be like," Mandie said, straightening her bonnet. Mrs. Taft had insisted that the girls wear their bonnets on deck. "And Paris. Do you think we might eventually meet Jonathan's aunt and uncle? Wouldn't that be fun?"

Celia frowned. "I don't know how, without your grandmother knowing everything."

"Still, I wonder what will happen to Jonathan when he gets off the boat in London," Mandie said. "Do you think he'll be able to contact his relatives in Paris before his father finds out where he is?"

"Maybe," Celia replied. "But his father will probably make him come home even if he does get to Paris. He said his father would never have allowed him to go there in the first place. I really don't know why he's so determined to go."

"Celia, I think—" Suddenly Mandie screamed, "Look out! There's Snowball."

Celia whirled around just in time to see the white kitten sailing out of the opened porthole. He landed hard on the deck and took off running.

Mandie chased him down the deck and finally caught him near the lifeboat where they had found Jonathan. Cuddling her kitten close, she shook her finger at him. "Oh, you naughty kitten," she scolded.

Snowball meowed pitifully.

"Mandie," Celia said with a worried tone in her voice, "this is the lifeboat that Jonathan stays in. And look! That man coming toward us is inspecting all the lifeboats."

Mandie looked up. The crewman was working only a few lifeboats away, straightening tarpaulins and tying them down.

"Let's wait here a minute," Mandie whispered. "The man is sure to find Jonathan, and even if he's not there, his valise is in the boat."

Celia nodded.

The girls moved back against the wall of the ship and watched. When the crewman approached the lifeboat Jonathan had been using, he lifted the tarpaulin and shook it out. The girls held their breath. But in a few seconds the crewman had finished tying down the tarpaulin and moved on to the next lifeboat.

"Whew!" Mandie exclaimed. "I was sure he was going

to find Jonathan, but evidently he didn't even find his valise. I wonder where that boy has moved to?"

"You got me!" Celia replied.

"Well, let's get this runaway kitten back in our room," Mandie said, leading the way.

When they returned to their cabin and opened the door, they both stood there in disbelief. Jonathan was sitting at the small table, hastily devouring a pile of food on a large plate. He hopped to his feet as soon as he saw them.

Mandie's temper flared. "Jonathan Guyer, what are you doing in our room?" she demanded.

Celia closed the door and Mandie let Snowball down.

Jonathan shrugged. "Since you couldn't bring me any more food, I just asked the steward to take some to your room, and this is what he brought," he said matter-of-factly.

"How did you know which room was ours?" Mandie asked with a sharp tone in her voice.

"I didn't, but I remembered you had a cat; and fortunately, when I was sneaking around the corridors, I heard it meow," Jonathan answered.

Mandie placed her hands firmly on her hips. "You know *better* than to go around doing things like that," she reprimanded. "You're going to get us in more hot water than we're already in."

"I'm sorry," Jonathan said flippantly. "I didn't think it would cause any trouble."

Mandie could feel her face getting redder. "Cause any trouble? Do you know what would happen if my grandmother found out about it?" she demanded.

"Besides, Jonathan, boys don't go into girls' rooms," Celia reminded him.

"That's right!" Mandie agreed. "You get out of our cabin right now, and don't ever come in here again!"

"All right. But I was so hungry...." Jonathan said sadly.

Mandie could feel her heart go out to him, but she knew she had to be firm. "I'm sorry you were hungry, but you agreed that you wouldn't ask us to do anything else to help you."

"Yes, I know. But do you know what it feels like to go a whole day without any food, especially when you can smell the delicious aroma coming from the galley and the dining room?" He shrugged again. "I guess you get it anyway you can." He thought for a minute then said, "I've never had to worry about food in my whole life, but now I understand how the poor feel when they don't have enough to eat."

"Don't confuse things, Jonathan," Mandie said. "It's one thing to be poor and unable to buy enough food, it's another to deliberately get yourself into the mess you've created."

"All right," the boy conceded. "I am sorry. I apologize, and I won't do it again."

Celia looked at Jonathan suspiciously. "Are you the one who took our bonbons and fruit yesterday?"

"I'm the one. I apologize for that too," he admitted. "Let me finish what's here and I'll leave."

He started to sit down again, but Mandie stopped him. "Don't sit again! You are not making yourself at home in our room. Hurry and finish, please."

Jonathan laughed. "Yes, ma'am!" he said. Picking up the plate, he pushed the rest of the food into his mouth.

Mandie noticed for the first time how bad the boy's clothes looked. "You look like you haven't changed clothes in a week!"

"And how do you think I would do that?" he replied. "I have no room or bath. But I promise you, as soon as we dock in London, I'll make haste to the nearest hotel to take a bath and change my clothes." He smiled smugly.

Mandie walked over to the door and opened it, gesturing for him to leave. "We'll see you in London," she said.

Jonathan walked past them and out into the corridor without another word.

Mandie was startled to see the strange woman in black standing in front of a door across the hall. She scurried away before Mandie could say anything.

"Oh no!" Mandie sighed. "If she saw Jonathan leave our room she will send another note to my grandmother!"

Celia closed the door. "I wish there was some way we could find out why she's so nosy."

Mandie dropped onto the little settee. "I do too, but she always disappears so quickly." She moved her feet and kicked something sticking out from under the settee.

Bending over to investigate, Mandie pulled out Jonathan's valise. "That ungrateful pest!" she cried, examining the expensive leather bag. "He's left his valise in our room! Why on earth would he do that?"

Celia leaned over Mandie's shoulder and looked at the bag. "That boy is unbelievable," she said. "I suppose he knew the man inspecting the lifeboats would have found it if he left it out there."

"No doubt," Mandie replied. "But that doesn't give him the right to stash it in our room!" She set the bag on the floor and kicked it with her shoe. "I've a good mind to just take it and throw it in some other lifeboat."

"That would be awfully mean," Celia said. "Jonathan might never find it again. I'd hate for him to lose all his things."

"All right," Mandie gave in. "But where can we hide it?" She looked around the tiny room. "There's not much room in here for anything as it is."

"How about just leaving it under the settee?" Celia suggested.

Mandie shook her head. "It's too easily seen under there." She kept looking around the room.

"How about in the clothes closet?"

"It might fit in there," Mandie said. Opening the sliding door to the small compartment, she lifted the valise to see if it would fit, but it wouldn't. "Too tight."

Celia looked around the room, worried. "I can't think of another place," she said.

"I know, Celia. There's a little cabinet under your bed." Taking the valise with her, she hurried over to the bunk and opened the sliding doors under Celia's bed. The space was empty. "It just happens we never thought to put anything in here," she said. "And it fits, see?" She put the bag inside.

Celia watched as Mandie slid the doors shut again. Satisfied that they had hidden the valise securely, they sat down again on the settee.

Mandie picked up Snowball and began stroking his silky fur. "I really do feel bad about Jonathan not getting much to eat," she said sadly.

"So do I," Celia admitted.

"Do you think we ought to try to take food to him again like we were doing before?" Mandie asked.

"I'm not sure, Mandie. What if we get caught?"

"We only have a few more days until we reach England," Mandie reminded her friend. "We wouldn't have to do it much longer."

"I'll go along with whatever you decide," Celia told her. "I'm really and truly sorry for Jonathan."

"All right, then, let's do it," Mandie decided. "Let's give him time to get settled back in the lifeboat, and then we can go talk to him."

"We'd better be sure that crewman has finished inspecting the boats," Celia cautioned.

"Oh yes. We'll go after lunch while most people are napping or spending time in their cabins," Mandie said.

That afternoon the girls took a stroll on the deck, looking for an opportunity to see Jonathan when no one was around. Walking up and down in the area of his lifeboat, they passed it several times, to see if he was there without drawing attention to themselves.

The sun beat down on them. "Oh, I wish these people would all go inside," she complained.

"It's so hot, I don't understand why they're all out here," Celia said.

As time passed, the girls grew tired from pacing the deck, but after a while the crowd thinned, and finally they were alone.

"Quick! Before someone else comes out. . . ." Mandie cautioned, hurrying to the lifeboat. Celia was right on her heels.

But just then a door burst open, and the little girl from the steerage section came running out onto the deck. The girls stopped in surprise.

The little girl darted toward the railing and Mandie and Celia sped after her.

"Violet!" Mandie called. "Don't go near that rail. You could fall overboard!"

The child turned, and looked at the girls and then took off again, ignoring their warnings.

Slowed by their long skirts, the girls chased her in circles. Then Violet headed straight to the railing next to the lifeboat Jonathan had been hiding in. She jumped up on the lower rung of the railing and looked back to see if the girls were following.

"Violet, get down! You'll fall into the water!" Mandie cried. When the little girl didn't move, Mandie ran toward her.

But just as she reached Violet, the child slipped between the lower railings and hurtled overboard.

Mandie and Celia screamed. Instantly, the deck was full of people. During the confusion, Jonathan popped out of his lifeboat and dived in after her.

A crowd gathered at the rail until a crewman ordered everyone back. "We've got to lower a lifeboat!" he cried.

Several other crewmen helped lower the lifeboat with a rescuer aboard.

Mandie's heart pounded. Celia squeezed her hand as they watched in horror from the railing. In the choppy water below Jonathan grabbed the little girl. He desperately clung to her, struggling to remain afloat in the high waves. Within minutes the lifeboat rowed up alongside him, and the crewmen pulled Violet into it. Jonathan clambered over the side and sat in the bottom of the lifeboat panting.

The crowd on the deck cheered as the boat was raised again. Celia and Mandie squealed with delight. But as soon as the lifeboat reached the deck, Jonathan jumped out and disappeared into the mob. Captain Montrose and the ship's doctor quickly arrived, and the crewmen lay Violet on the deck so that the doctor could examine her.

Mandie caught sight of Mrs. Taft and Senator Morton in the crowd. Nudging Celia, she nodded in their direction.

The doctor knelt beside Violet for a few moments, then looked up. "I think she'll be all right," he said. "She didn't take in much water thanks to the fellow who went in after her."

The captain stood and looked around. "Yes, where is that boy who rescued her?" he asked. "Where did he go?"

No one seemed to know. Then suddenly the strange woman in black stepped out of the crowd. "I know who that boy was," she announced haughtily. "He's the one I saw coming from the cabin of those girls there." She pointed toward Mandie and Celia.

Mrs. Taft quickly found her way over to the girls as they tried to shrink into the crowd. "Amanda, Celia, what is that woman talking about?"

Mandie looked down. "I don't know, Grandmother," she replied.

"We don't know that woman, Mrs. Taft," Celia volunteered.

"Amanda," Mrs. Taft persisted. "I'm asking you again. Was that woman talking about you two?" Getting no answer, she turned to the woman who had made the accusation. "Did you mean—?" But the woman had disappeared.

The captain called for silence. "Does anyone know who this child belongs to?" he asked loudly.

Mandie stepped forward. "Yes, sir," she answered immediately. "Her name is Violet Masterson, and she and her sister, Lily, are traveling in the steerage section."

Everyone gasped, and Mrs. Taft looked at her granddaughter sharply.

Captain Montrose raised his eyebrows. "And how do you know that, Miss Shaw?" he snapped.

The crowd hushed, and Violet began to cry softly.

Mandie knelt and hugged the drenched child protectively. "My kitten got out one day," she explained, "and we chased him down to the steerage section. This little girl found him. That's how we met her."

Senator Morton stepped out of the crowd. "So this is the child?" he said kindly.

"Yes, sir," Mandie replied, rocking Violet back and forth.

The captain smiled weakly at Mandie. "Thank you for identifying her," he said simply. Then calling over one of the crewmen who had helped in the rescue, he said, "Mr. Ganglinson, take this child back to steerage where she belongs, and tell her sister to make sure she doesn't come up here again," he said harshly.

"Aye, aye, sir." The robust man picked up Violet and carried her off toward the stairway.

Mandie expected the child to scream, but instead she seemed to like the man. She hugged his neck tightly.

Mrs. Taft put her hand on Mandie's shoulder. "Amanda, you'd better change your clothes," she said. "You are all wet from holding that child."

Mandie agreed and she and Celia hurried back to their cabin. "I half expect to find Jonathan in our room again," Mandie muttered as they walked down the long corridor.

"We should at least thank him for saving Violet," Celia reminded her.

Mandie nodded and opened the door to their room. No one was there.

Mandie quickly unbuttoned her wet dress and let it drop to the floor. "I wonder where he went?" she said.

Stepping out of the dress, she hung it up to dry.

As she went to the clothes closet, her eyes fell on the cabinet under the bunk. "Look, Celia," she cried. "The door to the cabinet is open." She ran over and looked inside. "And Jonathan's valise is gone."

Celia joined her and peered inside. "He *has* been in here! I suppose he needed some dry clothes, too."

"Well, he'd better not come back," Mandie said, sliding the door shut. Going back to the closet, she picked out a clean dress. "That strange woman has already made Grandmother suspicious."

"But he couldn't have gone back to the lifeboat with all those people out there," Celia reminded her.

"I know. Which means he has found some other place to hide," Mandie said, slipping on the lavender dress. "I wonder where?"

"We certainly can't take food to him unless we know where he is," Celia reasoned.

"It *was* courageous of him to jump off into the ocean and rescue Violet, wasn't it?" Mandie stood before the mirror, smoothing her dress. "If he hadn't been so quick, she probably would have drowned."

Celia nodded. "He gave himself away in order to save Violet," she said. "Now everyone is wondering who he is and where he got to."

"I suppose he's not such a bad fellow after all," Mandie agreed. Satisfied with her appearance, she headed for the door. "Let's go find him."

Chapter 9 / Help for Violet

Mandie and Celia checked his lifeboat, but Jonathan was not inside. Roaming all over the ship, they peered behind all the closed doors they dared open, and even checked behind the big settees in lounges where people were having tea. But they couldn't find him anywhere. Knowing it was almost time to dress for dinner, they started back to their cabin.

As they headed down the corridor to their room, they met their steward.

Mandie stopped him. "Charles, has the captain found the boy who rescued that little girl?" she asked.

"No, miss. I don't believe he has," Charles replied. "But then, don't you young ladies know the fellow?"

"Us?" Mandie asked innocently.

"He is the one who ordered food to your cabin, I'm sure," Charles told them.

Mandie and Celia looked at each other in desperation, not knowing what to say.

Just then Senator Morton emerged from his cabin and stopped to speak to them.

Mandie heaved a sigh of relief.

The senator smiled. "And how are the most beautiful young ladies on the ship?" he asked.

"We're fine, Senator Morton." Mandie smiled. "And by the way, thank you for those delicious bonbons."

Charles hurried on down the corridor.

Celia looked relieved. "Yes sir. That was so nice of you," she said.

"Sweets to the sweet, my dears," he said. "Well, I must be hurrying on. I have to speak to Mr. Holtzclaw about an important matter. I shall see you two at dinner."

"Yes, sir," the girls chimed in unison.

Inside their cabin, Celia took off her bonnet and tossed it on her bunk. "Mr. Holtzclaw," she repeated the name. "That's the newspaper man, isn't it?"

"Yes," Mandie replied. Flopping down on the settee, she took off her bonnet. "Oh, Celia, I'm so tired of this long boat ride. I wish I were home where I could see Uncle Ned, and Joe could help us solve all these mysteries."

Celia sat beside her friend. "I distinctly remember Joe warning you not to get mixed up in any adventures," she teased.

Mandie laughed. "He was just jealous that he wouldn't be along to get involved, too," she said. "But I'm glad Grandmother has been so busy with Senator Morton. Since she spends so much time with him, she doesn't have time to worry that much about what we're doing."

"She *is* giving us a lot of freedom," Celia agreed.

———

The next morning while Mrs. Taft was attending another lecture with the senator, Mandie and Celia searched again for Jonathan without success. As the girls moved about the ship, they heard some passengers who had witnessed the rescue talking about the possibility that the boy may have fallen back overboard and drowned.

As they returned to their cabin to freshen up for the noon meal, Mandie said, "I don't think Jonathan fell overboard, do you?"

Celia shook her head and started to say something, but just then there was a knock on the door.

Mandie answered it, and a crewman handed her a note.

Puzzled, Mandie frowned. "What is this?" she asked.

"It's from the sister of the little girl who almost drowned," the crewman explained.

"Oh, thank you," Mandie replied as the man left. Closing the door, she quickly unfolded the note.

Celia came and stood next to her as Mandie read aloud:

Dear Miss Mandie Shaw,

I thank you with all my heart for taking care of my little sister. She told me you let the captain know who she was so he could send her back to me. Please also give my deepest thanks to the boy who rescued her. I regret to inform you, though, that Violet tossed and turned all night with a high fever. She is awfully sick. I can only pray, and I trust that you and your friends will join me.

Eternally grateful,
Lily Masterson

Mandie looked up, her eyes moist. "Celia, Violet is desperately ill," she gasped. "Let's go down and see her!" They raced out the door and hurried down to the steerage section to see their little friend.

As they made their way down the endless flights of

steps, Mandie hoped they wouldn't get lost. Within a few minutes, however, they came out on the steerage deck. Some of the passengers spotted them, and a hush fell on the crowd.

Mandie rushed over to a shabbily dressed old woman. "Where is Lily Masterson?" she asked. "I want to see her little sister."

The woman didn't answer but merely pointed to her left. The girls hurried in that direction and found Violet lying on a pile of old quilts.

Lily sat on the floor beside her, bathing the child's face with a wet cloth. She looked up. "You shouldn't have come down here," she protested.

"I had to see if there was anything I can do for Violet," Mandie said. Suddenly she saw a boy coming toward them with a bucket of water. "Jonathan!" she exclaimed. "What are you doing here? We've been looking all over for you!"

"I heard the child was sick, and I came to see if I could do anything," he said meekly.

Mandie stooped down to touch Violet's flushed face. Though her eyes were open, she didn't seem to focus on anything. "Oh, Violet, you've got to get well!"

Lily began to bathe Violet's face and arms with the cool water Jonathan had brought. "I don't know what else to do," she said helplessly.

"I know one thing we can do," Mandie said boldly. Those gathered around became attentive and listened. "We can all pray for little Violet—every one of us."

Most of the people nodded in agreement, but a few mumbled and moved away, shaking their heads.

Mandie turned to Jonathan. "Jonathan, do you know how to lead a prayer?" she asked.

Jonathan looked puzzled. "Me? I don't think I know what you mean."

"All right," Mandie said resolvedly. "I'll do it then." Raising her voice, she said, "Let's all kneel right here and ask God to heal Violet." She watched and waited. People began dropping to their knees, one by one, until only a few at the other end of the deck remained standing. Jonathan just stood there, looking bewildered.

Mandie frowned at him. "Jonathan, can't you kneel?" she muttered, pulling on his shirtsleeve.

Mandie cleared her throat and was about to lead in prayer, when scores of voices could be heard, each one in his own way, calling on God to heal the little girl.

Mandie and Celia joined hands, and Mandie whispered, "Don't you think our favorite verse would apply in this situation?"

Her friend nodded vigorously.

"Jonathan," Mandie said, "say it with us."

He nodded and waited.

Lifting her face toward the sky, Mandie prayed the scripture, "What time I am afraid, I will put my trust in Thee."

Jonathan closed his eyes and said the verse with the girls as they repeated it.

Mandie reached over and squeezed Lily's hand. "Dear Lord, please heal little Violet," she continued. "Please make her well and strong again. Soothe her misery and cool her fever. And, dear Lord, please help Lily to be brave. We thank you, Lord. Amen."

Mandie looked around at her friends. They were all smiling.

Mandie felt sure that the Lord had heard and would heal Violet. She had also made a big decision. She would ask Grandmother to help the Mastersons, but she didn't tell the girls her plans.

"Lily, we've got to go now," Mandie said, getting to her feet.

Lily looked up. Tears began to fill her blue eyes. "Thank you," she managed.

"Come on, Celia. Are you coming too, Jonathan?" Mandie asked. "Let's find my grandmother." The three hurried toward the steps.

Jonathan stopped in his tracks. "Your grandmother? You know I can't be seen on the ship."

"Well, how did you get down to the steerage?" Mandie asked.

"That's different." Jonathan shrugged. "These people don't care who I am. They don't pay any attention to me. I'm just one of them, as far as they can judge."

"Have you been staying down here since you rescued Violet?" Celia asked.

"No, I had just got here when you two came down," he replied. "I suppose you'll find out sooner or later. I found an empty cabin, and I've been staying in it."

Mandie's eyes grew wide. "An empty cabin?"

"Sh-h-h! Not so loud! Don't tell everyone on the ship," Jonathan warned. "Yes, an empty cabin. But it's nowhere near yours."

Celia took Mandie's arm. "He's right, Mandie," she said. "He really shouldn't be seen. Remember, he's still a stowaway."

"All right. Go back to your empty cabin," Mandie said. "Come on, Celia. I want to talk to my grandmother."

Jonathan followed the girls up the steps, and when they turned at the top landing, he went in the opposite direction. Mandie didn't pay any attention to where he went, she was in too much of a hurry.

A short time later the girls found Mrs. Taft and the senator in the music room, listening to an opera singer.

Celia remained at the door as Mandie made her way through the crowd.

Approaching her grandmother, who was sitting at the end of a row, Mandie bent over to whisper, "Grandmother, I need to talk to you. It's urgent."

Mrs. Taft looked alarmed. Turning to the senator, she said, "Will you excuse me, please?"

"Of course," said Senator Morton. "In fact, I'll go with you. I'm not enjoying this anyway." He followed them from the room.

In the hallway, Mandie immediately told her grandmother about Violet's illness. "And she doesn't have a doctor or even a bed to sleep on. It's absolutely horrible down there," she wailed. "If you will just come down and see for yourself, I know you'll agree that the girls need help. Please?"

"Amanda," Mrs. Taft was firm, "didn't I tell you not to go down to the steerage again? You have disobeyed me."

"I know, Grandmother, and I'm sorry," Mandie replied. "I didn't intend to deliberately disobey you, but that little girl might die if she doesn't get some help." She fought back tears.

"Violet *is* terribly sick, Mrs. Taft," Celia confirmed.

"I would be glad to go down there and investigate for you," Senator Morton volunteered. "I don't want to interfere with your affairs, but maybe I could help in some way."

Mrs. Taft just stood there for a moment, looking at the senator. Mandie held her breath, waiting to see what her grandmother would do.

Finally she heaved a big sigh. "All right. I'll go with you," she said.

Mandie glanced at Celia and smiled. She was sure now that her grandmother would get help for Violet. She led the way as they all headed down to the steerage section.

Reaching the bottom of the stairs, Mrs. Taft stopped short to survey the crowded deck. "Oh, my!" she gasped. "I had no idea there were so many people down here."

"The Mastersons are over this way," Mandie said, taking the lead through the crowd.

Everyone around them stared at Mrs. Taft and Senator Morton.

Approaching Lily, Mandie introduced her to the adults. "You see how sick Violet is, Grandmother?" she said. She knelt beside the child as Lily stared, red-eyed at the well-dressed strangers.

To Mandie's surprise, her grandmother, in spite of her layers of underskirts and outer skirts, managed to stoop down next to the child. "How long has she been this ill?" Mrs. Taft asked Lily.

"Since last night, ma'am," Lily replied, stifling a sob. "And I have done everything I know to do for her."

"Well, there is something else we can do," Mrs. Taft said sternly. She held her hand up to the senator for assistance in rising. Smoothing her skirts, she turned to a crewman working on a hose nearby. "Mister, we need your assistance here," she said.

The crewman looked up, surprised to see people who were obviously from the first-class section of the ship. "Uh, yes, ma'am, what can I do for you?"

"Would you please go find the captain for me, and tell him he is urgently needed down here!" she ordered.

"You can tell him Mrs. Taft asked for him."

"Yes, ma'am!" He bowed slightly, and rushed off, taking the steps in great strides.

In a few minutes, he returned with Captain Montrose.

The captain looked surprised to see the girls and the senator. "Yes, Mrs. Taft. You sent for me?" He glanced at the child lying on the floor.

"Yes, sir," Mrs. Taft replied. "It seems the child who fell overboard has contracted a high fever. I want this child moved to the sick bay at once so that the ship's doctor can take care of her."

"But, madam, this is the steerage section," Captain Montrose objected. "No provision is made for medical care for these people."

"I don't care what provision is made for them." Mrs. Taft stretched to her full height. "I want this child moved to the sick bay immediately!" she demanded. "She's so sick she's liable to die lying there on that floor."

"Mrs. Taft, you must be reasonable," the captain protested.

Senator Morton cleared his throat. "I don't think you understand, Captain. We are being reasonable," he said. "That child's life is in danger, and we must do something about it. Now!"

Mandie and Celia listened in amazement. Lily stared, her mouth open.

"Sir, I have no authority to move a steerage passenger to the first-class medical facility," the captain held his ground.

Mrs. Taft was livid. "Do you want me to go upstairs and speak to the other first-class passengers? Many of them witnessed the rescue of this child from certain death when she fell overboard. Do you want me to tell them you refused a doctor's care for her now that she is deathly ill with a fever? Someone might be enraged enough to say that the accident was your fault."

"My fault?" The captain was beginning to look nervous. "I had nothing to do with the accident."

Mandie spoke up. "Captain Montrose, when my grandmother makes up her mind to do something, no one can stop her."

The captain looked at Mandie, and finally gave in. "All right." He raised his arms in a helpless gesture. "You win." He summoned the crewman working on the hose. "Take this child to the sick bay immediately, and tell the doctor I said to take care of her."

"Aye, captain," the man said and bent to lift Violet in his strong arms. The captain quickly walked away toward the steps.

Lily stood up, crying. Mrs. Taft put her arm around the girl's shoulders and told her, "Get your things. You have to stay with her to be sure they do their job."

"Me go, too? That captain might not like that," Lily protested as she sobbed.

"Leave the captain to me, dear. Get your things," Mrs. Taft insisted.

Lily quickly picked up a bag sitting nearby and turned to an old woman who stood listening. "Mrs. White, would you please watch out for my other belongings while I'm gone?"

"Of course, dear, and we'll all be praying for little Violet," Mrs. White told her.

"Let's go," Mrs. Taft told the crew member who had been standing there holding the child all this time.

When they came to the corridor leading to their cabin Mrs. Taft told Lily, "You go that direction now. Follow the man. I'll see that you're provided with food and a place to sleep so you can watch over your little sister. Hurry on, dear. We'll be stopping in to check on her."

"Oh, thank you, thank you," Lily said, quickly squeezing Mrs. Taft's hand and hurrying after the man carrying Violet.

"Grandmother, I'm sorry if I disobeyed you, but you can see what you think about it. If I had not gone down to check on Violet you wouldn't know about it and she might have died for want of attention," Mandie told her grandmother at the door of Mrs. Taft's cabin.

"I understand, dear. I forgive you. You girls will have to keep check on what goes on in the sick bay and let me know," Mrs. Taft told them.

Senator Morton had crossed the hall to enter his cabin.

"And we thank you, Senator Morton," Mandie called to him.

"I didn't do a thing," he protested. "It was your grandmother who got the ball rolling. Now it's up to you girls to see that the ball keeps on rolling."

"Yes, sir," the girls chimed.

As the girls entered their cabin and closed the door Mandie said, "I knew my grandmother would come through."

"Like she did for Hilda that time," Celia agreed.

"We'd better get going, or we'll be late for dinner," Mandie reminded her. "And you know Grandmother didn't even mention that it's almost time to eat. Even if it meant losing out on a meal, I knew she would take care of Violet first."

Chapter 10 / Lady Detective on Board

In the next couple of days Mandie and Celia spent a lot of time with Lily and Violet in the sick bay. With the proper medical attention the child had begun to improve.

On the third day, when the fever finally broke, Violet opened her eyes and cried, "Lily, I'm hungry!"

Overjoyed at the good sign, Lily hugged the child, and smiled warmly at Mandie and Celia who had come to visit.

Celia squeezed Mandie's hand. "Violet's going to get well," she said excitedly.

"I knew she would." Mandie dabbed at her moist eyes with her handkerchief.

Violet struggled to sit up but was too weak. Then glancing at Mandie and Celia, she frowned. "Where are we?"

The girls all began talking at once, trying to explain to the child where they were and why. Just then the doctor came in to check on Violet. Seeing that she was alert, he ordered some broth for her. "I'll be back shortly," he promised.

A steward arrived with the broth, and Lily began feeding the warm nourishment to her sister. After a few spoonfuls, Violet drifted off to sleep again. "Well, I guess we'll have to go back downstairs now that Violet is recovering," Lily told Mandie.

"Oh no," Mandie protested. "I'm sure you should stay right here. Let me talk to my grandmother. She will verify it with the captain. We only have two more days before we get to London!"

"I don't want to cause any trouble." Lily looked worried.

"It's no trouble," Mandie said. "It's important that Violet get some good rest in a proper bed until she is completely well. You can't worry about what people think."

"Well, at least the captain hasn't been around," Lily sighed. "He frightens me. He's so—so stern and gruff. He would never have allowed us to come up here, if your grandmother hadn't intervened."

Lily leaned forward. "Did anyone ever find out who that boy was that saved Violet, or where he went?" she asked. "He seemed to just disappear."

Mandie looked at her in surprise. "You mean, you didn't know the boy who brought you the bucket of water for Violet was the one who'd rescued her?"

Lily gasped. "No! That boy?"

"He didn't say anything about it?" Celia asked.

Lily's blonde curls had become tangled and unruly with neglect, as she had been spending all her time caring for her sister. She pushed back the damp ringlets. "No, he just said he heard that Violet was ill, and came down to see if there was anything he could do," she explained.

"Well, that's surprising!" Mandie exclaimed.

"Do you two know him?" Lily asked. "No one seems to know where he went."

Mandie shrugged. "Not really." Then, changing the subject, "Is there anything we can do for you before we go, Lily?" She stood up.

"Oh no, thank you." Lily smiled. "You have done so much already. I appreciate it more than I can say."

"I'm so glad you sent that note, letting us know that Violet was sick," Mandie told her. "You'd better lie down now and get some rest. You'll need your strength when we get to London."

"I will," Lily promised.

"We'll see you again before we dock," Mandie said as the two left the room.

As they walked down the corridor, Mandie had another idea. "Why don't we see if we can find Jonathan?"

"He said he was in an empty cabin, remember?" Celia said. "How will we know which one, with all the doors closed?"

Mandie grabbed Celia's arm. "It's that strange woman," she whispered loudly, pointing to the cross hall ahead. The two girls hurried to see if they could follow her. When they got to the corner, they saw her heading outside to the deck.

She sat down in a deck chair and pulled a book out of the large bag she carried. Although she seemed oblivious to the girls presence on the deck, they stopped before they got closer.

"Let's just sit down in a couple of chairs near her and watch her the way she watches us," Mandie said.

Celia nodded.

Mandie led the way and they found chairs at just enough distance that they could whisper without being heard.

At first the woman seemed to be engrossed in her

book, but Mandie kept her eyes on her. A few minutes later, the woman glanced her way. Mandie just stared back.

Without dropping her eyes, Mandie struck up a conversation with Celia. "Two more days and we'll actually be in London!" she said excitedly.

"This sure has been a long trip." Celia rested her head back on the chair.

"But it has been exciting, too, don't you think?" Mandie asked. "The best part about going home again will be to tell Joe about our adventures."

Celia shook her head. "It will be a while before we see him again."

"I suppose Mother and Uncle John will be down at the Pattons in Charleston again when we get back."

"Mandie!" Celia threw her hands in the air. "We haven't even landed in London, and you're talking about getting back home. Are you homesick already?"

Mandie laughed. "Of course not. I'm anxious to see everything in Europe. I wouldn't even mind if we stayed the rest of the year."

"But we have to go back to school in September, and as it is, we'll barely make it back in time."

Mandie was still watching the woman in black, who had resumed reading. "I wonder if April Snow will be back to school in the fall," she said.

"You know, school would be a lot more pleasant if April Snow would just decide to go to another school," Celia replied.

Mandie laughed again. "But then we wouldn't have any troublemakers to contend with."

"I suppose it would take all the excitement out of being at school." Celia giggled.

Mandie giggled too, forgetting to keep her eyes on the reason they were sitting on the deck in the first place. When she finally looked up, the woman was gone. "Celia, she's disappeared again!"

The girls jumped up and looked around. Mandie shook her head. "I look away for a few seconds and she's gone!"

Celia straightened her skirt. "She's a clever one all right."

"Come on, let's take a stroll," Mandie suggested.

Noticing that most of the deck chairs were empty now, Mandie looked at the pendant watch on the chain around her neck. "We have just fifteen minutes before we meet Grandmother for the noon meal," she said.

They paused near the lifeboat where Jonathan had been staying before all the recent events.

Celia nodded toward the boat. "Do you think Jonathan might possibly be in there?" she asked.

"I don't know why, but it wouldn't hurt to check," Mandie replied. "Let's see." Walking over to the lifeboat, she slapped the side of it. "Hey, are you there?" she asked.

To the girls' surprise, Jonathan popped his head out from under the tarpaulin, and jumped down to greet them.

"Here we've been looking all over the ship for you, and you've gone back to the lifeboat," Mandie fussed.

Jonathan smiled. "Why were you looking for me?"

"We own a part of you, remember?" Mandie teased. "If we lose track of you completely, we won't be able to collect that reward!"

Jonathan laughed. "So, you're really after my money, after all, huh?"

Celia frowned. "You're not very funny," she said.

"No, you're not," Mandie agreed. "It was *your* idea. If we turned you in to the captain, we wouldn't bother collecting the reward, but you promised it to us for the Cherokee school. I must say, you certainly have a short memory."

"I haven't forgotten," Jonathan assured them. "I was only teasing you. If we don't see each other again before we get into port, then I'll find you when the ship docks."

"You'd better," Mandie said. "Say, in case you are interested, Violet is much better now. Her fever has broken, and she was eating some broth this morning." She straightened her bonnet. "By the way, why didn't you tell Lily that you were the one who rescued Violet?"

Jonathan looked down, suddenly shy. "Why should I? It doesn't matter who rescued the little girl. What matters is that she is alive and well."

"You're right." Mandie smiled.

"Why did you leave that empty cabin you were staying in?" Celia asked.

Jonathan grinned. "I almost got caught when the maids cleaned the rooms this morning," he replied. "Fortunately, there happened to be a connecting door to the next cabin, and it was unlocked, so I slipped out that way."

"I'll bet you're glad that we only have two more days on this ship," Mandie remarked.

He nodded.

Celia ran her hand along the ship's railing. "We'll sure be glad to get away from that strange woman who keeps snooping around us," she said.

Jonathan raised his eyebrows. "Strange woman? Who's that?"

"You know, the one who tried to point you out when you rescued the little girl," Celia explained.

"I heard someone say something, but I really didn't see her," Jonathan replied. "There were so many people around, I ducked out real fast. What does she look like?"

"She's old and scrawny looking, and she wears black all the time," Celia answered.

"She's real short—shorter than I am. And she has lots of diamond rings on her fingers, and she wears an enormous brooch on her blouse," Mandie added. "Her bonnet completely covers her hair, but one day when the wind was blowing, I noticed some wisps of gray."

"Hmm!" Jonathan mused. "You say she's been spying on you? Like how, exactly?"

"Well, I know she must be the one who sent an anonymous note to my grandmother, telling her that we weren't behaving like young ladies should," Mandie said. "And she always seems to be hovering around our hallway and cabin. Today she watched us from a deck chair."

"But we've never seen her in the dining room, so she must eat at another seating," Celia told him.

Jonathan frowned. "I don't think I've ever seen her."

Mandie glanced at her watch again. "We've got to go, now, Jonathan. Is this where you're going to be staying then?"

"Looks like it," he said with a sigh. "I left my valise in a hall closet near your room."

Mandie gasped. "Someone will find it!"

"No, I don't think so," he said. "I put it inside the wall where the water trap opens."

"I hope it's there when you go back," Mandie said, shaking her head. She turned to go and waved. "We'll see you later."

Jonathan climbed back into the boat and pulled the

tarpaulin over his head, and the girls headed back to their cabin.

At the noon meal the girls visited with Mandie's grandmother and Senator Morton while waiting to be served. Mrs. Taft leaned forward. "I know you girls will enjoy hearing this," she said barely above a whisper. "They say there's a real lady detective on this ship. Can you imagine? A *woman* detective?"

Celia gasped. "Really? What does she look like?"

Mandie was sure Celia was thinking what she was thinking—the strange woman just may have an identity after all.

"I have no idea, dear," Mrs. Taft replied. She turned to the senator. "Have you seen her?"

"No, I don't believe so," he replied. "They say she's just ordinary looking, though. You wouldn't know she was a detective. But then, who would know what a lady detective should look like?" He smiled.

"Well, if y'all find out, I'd sure like to know," Mandie said. "That is, I think it would be real interesting to meet a lady detective." She didn't want to sound too worried. Jonathan could be in for some real trouble if that woman found out about him.

Celia shot her a knowing glance.

Mandie and Celia commented about Violet's recovery, and Mrs. Taft smiled happily.

"I am delighted to hear that the little girl is better," she said. "I'll have to see to it that she and her sister are allowed to stay in the sick bay until we get to London. That place downstairs is horribly overcrowded. In fact, I think I shall do something about it."

"Like what, Grandmother?" Mandie didn't want to give away the fact that she knew who owned the ship.

"The captain of a ship is supposed to be responsible for such things," she said indignantly. "The ship's order and condition is given to his charge. He should have certain rules and regulations to protect all passengers, whether they pay first-class fares or not."

"But isn't the shipping line that owns the ship the one that sets the fares and the number of passengers allowed and all that?" Mandie observed her grandmother's reaction.

"Sometimes the owner may not know exactly what goes on, Mandie. Employees are paid to run the business for the owner," Mrs. Taft replied.

"I'm sure if the owner of this ship knew what things were like down there, conditions would improve," Mandie said with a smile.

"You're absolutely right," Mrs. Taft agreed.

Just then the waiter brought their food, and the conversation switched to other topics.

About halfway through their meal, Mr. Holtzclaw, the newspaper man, came by the table and the senator invited him to join them.

"Yes, please do," Mrs. Taft insisted.

Mr. Holtzclaw pulled over a chair from another table and sat next to the senator. "This could wait, but I just wanted to bring you up-to-date on that kidnapping in New York—you know, Lindall Guyer's son," he said.

The senator nodded and continued eating.

"I was able to contact my New York office on the wireless this morning," Mr. Holtzclaw continued, "and the latest news is that the reward has been doubled."

Mandie and Celia looked at each other and tried to hide their surprise.

"I sure hope Lindall finds the boy," Senator Morton

replied. "It must be very difficult for him."

"Well, in a way it's the man's own fault. He has really neglected the boy," Mr. Holtzclaw explained. "He keeps him in private schools all the time, not giving the boy a chance to get to know his father very well." He scratched his forehead, thinking for a moment. "You know, I've never even met the boy. He's been away at school whenever I've been at their house. But I understand he gets high marks in school."

Mandie bit her lip to keep from saying anything.

Senator Morton wiped his mouth with his napkin. "I believe his mother is dead, isn't she?"

"That's right. She died when he was a baby," Mr. Holtzclaw replied.

Mrs. Taft set down her fork and looked from the senator to Mr. Holtzclaw and back again. "Is he the multimillionaire in New York who tries to buy out everybody's businesses?" she asked coldly.

Mr. Holtzclaw laughed. "You've got him pegged right. He tries to buy anything he thinks will make money for him, and he usually succeeds because he's got the money to pay for it."

"Well, money doesn't buy everything," Mrs. Taft commented. "I am sure there are those people who want to keep their business because it has been in the family a long time. Others don't need the money, and won't sell no matter what is offered."

"That's true," Mr. Holtzclaw said, standing. "But I must be going now. Have a good afternoon."

Senator Morton nodded to him. "Let me know if you hear anything further," he said.

"I will do that," Mr. Holtzclaw promised.

Mrs. Taft laid her hand on Senator Morton's arm. "Do

you suppose someone kidnapped Mr. Guyer's son for the money, or to settle the score on a sour business deal?" she asked.

"The paper said they *assume* he's been kidnapped," the senator emphasized. "It wouldn't surprise me if he's run away."

Mrs. Taft gasped. "Oh, dear! I hadn't thought of that."

Mandie felt guilty, knowing about Jonathan and not reporting his whereabouts to Mr. Holtzclaw. The news could be gotten to Jonathan's father in minutes via the wireless.

Her face felt hot as she debated what to do. Finally she decided to talk to Jonathan again and tell him that she felt she should let his father know where he was. As soon as she and Celia could get away, she would try to see him at the lifeboat.

But what if that lady detective is looking for him? she thought. She brushed the idea aside. She was sure no one knew Jonathan was on the ship except her and Celia. Besides, the woman seemed to be following them, not looking for someone else. Surely the strange woman was the detective her grandmother had told them about. *But why would a detective be bothering about us?* she argued with herself. *Everything is so complicated!*

Mrs. Taft insisted that the girls go with her and the senator to the lounge for dessert and coffee. Mandie and Celia were reluctant, but didn't know how to get out of it.

As soon as they could get away, they went out on deck and waited for an opportunity to talk to Jonathan. It was late afternoon before the crowd thinned out and Mandie and Celia could approach the lifeboat without worrying about being discovered.

They hurried over to the boat and called out to him. There was no answer.

Mandie tapped lightly on the side of the lifeboat. "Are you there?" she asked, afraid to use his name in case someone might be within hearing range.

Still no answer.

Celia shrugged. "He's not here," she said.

"I wonder where he could be this time," Mandie said, disappointed. "Just when we really need to talk to him, he's not here."

Celia tapped Mandie on the shoulder. "Some people are coming out for a stroll," she warned, watching the door to the cabin area.

Mandie turned away from the lifeboat. "We can try again after a while," she said. "He's going to get caught sooner or later, the way he runs around all over the ship."

"That's what I've been thinking, too," Celia said as they walked on down the deck.

"And if somebody else catches him, we won't be able to collect the reward money to help build the Cherokee school," Mandie added. "And after all the trouble we've been through for him!"

Chapter 11 / "You Are the One!"

After dinner that night, Mandie and Celia excused themselves early and tried finding Jonathan again. Since most people were still eating, there was no one on deck, and Mandie tapped on the lifeboat. "Hey, are you in there?" she said in a loud whisper.

The boy lifted the tarpaulin, always eager for a reason to escape his tiny home, and climbed out to talk to them.

"Jonathan, you may be in real trouble," Mandie began. "Do you know a Mr. Holtzclaw? He owns the newspaper I showed you with the article about your disappearance."

"My father knows the man," Jonathan replied. "I've never seen him. Why?"

"Well, he told my grandmother and the senator that he had contacted his newspaper by wireless and that your father has doubled the reward!"

Jonathan was unimpressed, and simply grinned. "That means you girls will be twice as rich!"

Celia scowled. "Wait a minute. That's not all," she said. "Mrs. Taft told us there's a lady detective on this ship!"

"We think it might be that strange woman who's always following us around, spying on us," Mandie added. "We haven't been able to figure out why she follows us. Do you think she might be looking for you?"

"Hmm!" Jonathan thought for a moment, then said, "Why would she be looking for me when no one knows I got on this ship but you girls?"

"Well, I thought we were the only ones who knew," Mandie said, "but maybe someone else does know. How can we be sure?"

"It's impossible," Jonathan argued. "I boarded the ship in Charleston, not New York. In fact, I hitchhiked all the way to Charleston because I was afraid someone would recognize me in New York."

"Where did you stay in Charleston?" Celia asked.

"Nowhere. I just walked down to the pier as soon as I arrived, and this ship was docking. I managed to sneak on board right away," he explained. "It was almost dark."

Mandie sighed. "Why won't you let us contact your father and tell him where you are?" she persisted. "We could ask Mr. Holtzclaw to send him a message on the wireless through his newspaper."

"No, no, no!" Jonathan shook his head vigorously. "You can't do that!"

"But as soon as your father finds out you're in Paris, he'll just order you home anyway," Celia argued.

"When I get to Paris, I'll have my aunt and uncle behind me. My father might listen to them." The wind ruffled his curly black hair, and he smoothed it into place. "Anyway, I'll take that chance."

Mandie's blue eyes narrowed. "I feel so badly, knowing that your father is up there in New York worrying about you," she said.

"I doubt if he's worrying too much about me. He only has time for his business," Jonathan said sarcastically. "He never has liked children. They're too much trouble. I don't care if I ever see him again, to be honest."

"Jonathan!" Mandie exclaimed. "Don't you love your father?"

Jonathan shuffled his feet and looked out over the ocean. "How can you love someone you don't even know?"

Celia gasped. "You don't know your father?"

"Well, of course I recognize him when I see him, which is very seldom," the boy replied. "But as I said before, he sends me away to private schools. I've never been with him long enough to get to know him. It's obvious he just doesn't want me around, so I decided to fend for myself."

Mandie looked into his dark eyes and reached out to him. "I'm sorry, Jonathan, but I can tell you love your father, even though you say you don't," she said gently. "Why don't you just have a good man-to-man talk with him? That might straighten things out between you."

"A man-to-man talk?" the boy laughed lightly. "My father wouldn't have time for such a thing. In fact, I doubt if he has ever had a good personal talk with anyone. I really don't know what my mother ever saw in him."

Mandie looked up just in time to see the strange woman "detective" coming toward them across the deck. She was moving too quickly for them to do anything to hide Jonathan. Mandie's heart pounded.

"You are the one!" the woman shouted, pointing a bony finger at Jonathan.

Startled at her outburst, he just stared at her for a moment. "Ma'am?" he finally managed.

The girls were too stunned to speak.

"You are the one," the strange woman repeated loudly. "I would recognize you anywhere!"

Recognize him? Mandie thought to herself. *Does she know who he is?* To her utter dismay, Mandie noticed her grandmother and Senator Morton approaching, along with other people who were now leaving the dining room.

"Go!" she warned Jonathan, "Disappear into the crowd." But he didn't move.

As Mrs. Taft and the senator approached, the woman began accusing Jonathan again, "You are the one I saw coming out of these girls' cabin that day!"

"Amanda! What is this?" Grandmother Taft looked shocked. "What is going on here?"

"I ... I ... don't know," Mandie was temporarily speechless. "We—we don't even know this woman." She turned to her then. "Just who are you, anyway, ma'am?"

Before she could answer, Mandie's grandmother had another question, "And who is this young man that she accuses of being in your cabin?"

Jonathan rolled his eyes. "We can explain, ma'am," he said. "It's all very simple."

"You *will* explain," Mrs. Taft said firmly.

"Grandmother," Mandie said calmly, "could we all sit down on some deck chairs and talk? We can explain everything."

The curious crowd that had gathered dispersed, deciding there was nothing so unusual going on. But the unidentified woman in black stayed close behind Mandie.

Mrs. Taft addressed her abruptly, "I don't believe this concerns you any longer."

The woman hurried away in a huff.

Mandie waited until the others were seated, then

faced them in a chair of her own. "Grandmother," she began rather nervously, "this boy is a stowaway and—"

"What? A stowaway?" Senator Morton scowled. "He'll have to be reported to the captain!"

"Please don't, sir," Jonathan begged. "We're almost to London. I'll get off the ship there, and I won't cause anyone any more bother."

Mrs. Taft bristled. "Young man, you are far too young to be traveling alone, much less stowing away on a ship!"

"Oh, Grandmother, please don't report him," Mandie pleaded. "He hasn't done anything wrong, really. When he gets to London, he can get the money to pay for his passage."

"Hasn't done anything wrong?" Mrs. Taft stared at her in disbelief. "Please explain what that woman meant when she said she saw him coming out of your cabin, then."

"He was hungry," Mandie replied. "He hasn't been anything but a gentleman with us, has he, Celia?"

"That's right," Celia agreed. "In fact, he stays hidden most of the time and doesn't bother anyone."

Jonathan leaned forward in his deck chair. "If you would just forget you ever saw me, I'd be so grateful, ma'am," he said. "I can assure you I won't go into the girls' cabin again."

Mrs. Taft looked at the boy sternly. "But it remains that you have broken the law by stowing away on this ship, without passage. Didn't you know that?"

"I know I shouldn't have boarded this ship without paying the passenger fare, but it was an urgent situation, and I couldn't get my hands on any money right then," Jonathan explained.

Mrs. Taft laughed lightly. "I can believe that! You are too young to be in command of any money." She looked at Senator Morton for advice. "Do you think we should take him to Captain Montrose?"

The senator cleared his throat. "According to the law, that is our obligation," he answered. "But you know, the girls have also broken the law by concealing a runaway."

Mandie and Celia both gasped. Mandie cringed at the thought of punishment at the hand of the captain.

Mrs. Taft drummed her fingers on her handbag in her lap. "Amanda, the thing that concerns me almost more is that you and Celia have deceived me, and I cannot let that go unpunished."

The girls bowed their heads, suddenly acknowledging their wrongdoing to Mrs. Taft. "Yes, ma'am," Mandie said for them both.

"You must realize that I will have to tell both your mothers about all of this, don't you?"

Mandie couldn't look her grandmother in the face. "I'm truly sorry," she said quietly.

"So am I," Celia added. "I am certain nothing like this will ever happen again."

Jonathan stood then. "You know, Mrs. Taft, this whole thing is all my fault," he admitted. "I should never have involved the girls in my problem. I'm sorry for the trouble I've caused your family."

The senator stood beside the boy and helped Mrs. Taft to her feet. "Shall we all go find the captain?"

"Grandmother!" Mandie exclaimed. "I've just realized, you probably aren't aware who this boy is!"

Celia caught her breath. "That's right!" she said. "He's the one who rescued the little girl who fell overboard!"

"What? You?" Mrs. Taft turned to the boy. "You saved that little girl's life?"

Jonathan was suddenly embarrassed at the attention.

"Well, I only did what any other person would do under the circumstances."

"That gives us two reasons to take you to the captain," she replied. "Captain Montrose has been looking for the person that rescued the girl. Come along now, we'll go find him."

Mrs. Taft led the way inside and down the long corridor. They passed the sick bay on the way to the captain's quarters, and Mrs. Taft peeked in the doorway. "We might as well see how little Violet is doing, now that we're here," she said. She and Senator Morton entered the tiny room while the others waited by the door.

They found the child sitting on her cot while Lily read a book to her. The two looked up when the visitors entered.

Mrs. Taft reached out to the little girl and touched her cheek. "How are you, my dear?"

"I've been sick," the little girl replied, shyly, looking at her sister. "But I'm better now."

"Yes, and we're so glad you're doing well," Mrs. Taft told her, smiling.

Lily spoke then. "She is much, much better, Mrs. Taft, thanks to your kindness and quick action. She's eating solid food now, so she's getting much stronger."

Mrs. Taft opened the drawstring of her purse and pulled out a piece of paper and a pencil. "I want to get the address of the place where you'll be staying in London," she said. "Would you write it here for me?"

"Of course."

"And I want to give you money to buy a kitten for Violet," Mrs. Taft continued. "A white one, if you can find one."

Violet beamed. "A kitten? For me?"

"Yes, dear, as soon as your sister can find you one," Mrs. Taft spoke kindly. Taking several bills from her bag, she gave them to Lily. "This ought to be enough."

Lily took the money shyly, and handed her their address in London. "Mrs. Taft, I don't know how I can ever repay you. I'm hopelessly in your debt."

"Don't mention it, please. It was a pleasure doing something for somebody who really needed it, for a change," she said, squeezing Lily's hand. "You just see that your little sister gets a kitten."

Lily finally noticed the girls at the door, and then Jonathan. "Oh, you're the boy who saved my sister's life!" she exclaimed. "I just wanted to—"

Suddenly Jonathan bolted and ran, disappearing down the corridor.

Mandie looked bewilderedly at her grandmother. "Shall Celia and I go look for him?" she asked.

Mrs. Taft sighed. "No dear. Let him go," she said. "Perhaps he deserves free passage for saving a life. I don't think we should pursue him."

Mandie and Celia exchanged glances and took a deep breath.

"But I think you girls should leave him alone, if you do see him the rest of the trip," Grandmother Taft warned.

"Yes, ma'am!" Mandie was relieved that Jonathan had gotten away.

Lily reached for Mrs. Taft's hand. "But ma'am, you know Captain Montrose has been looking everywhere for the boy. I believe he wants to give him some kind of reward for rescuing Violet."

At that moment the captain walked into the sick bay through another door. "Did I hear my name mentioned?

What can I do for you?" he said, looking to Mrs. Taft.

"Captain Montrose, I'm glad you're here. It happens that we have found the young boy who saved Violet's life," Mrs. Taft told him.

"Oh? Where is he? I wanted to do something for him," the captain replied. "I've had my crewmen looking everywhere for him."

Mrs. Taft drew herself up to her full height. "Well, the reason they have not been able to find him is because he is a stowaway, and—"

"A stowaway?" the captain interrupted, his face reddening. "That scoundrel! Where has he been hiding?"

Mandie and Celia trembled and held hands. The captain could be so frightening when he was angry.

But Mrs. Taft stood up to him. "Well, he is most certainly on this ship, but I couldn't tell you where he is hiding because I don't know."

"Are you sure of that, Mrs. Taft?" Captain Montrose looked like he didn't believe her. "It's against the law to harbor runaways, you know. Where did you find him in the first place?"

Senator Morton spoke up. "He was outside on the deck, and he came with us to see how little Violet was doing," he said matter-of-factly. "Evidently you scared him off."

Mandie sighed with relief, glad that her grandmother and the senator were protecting Jonathan. She secretly hoped the boy could stay hidden until the ship docked in London.

"If you see him again, it is your duty to inform me," the captain said sharply.

"Maybe your crew will find him," Mrs. Taft said smugly. "Come along, girls. It's time we go." Turning to Lily and

Violet, she said, "Have a good day now, we will see you again."

Mandie and Celia backed out of the small room and bumped into the strange woman. It was apparent she had heard everything at the door.

The woman barged through the doorway and spoke directly to the captain. "These girls know that boy," she insisted. "Just ask them. They know who he is."

Mrs. Taft stepped between the woman and the captain. "I wish you would leave these girls alone," she said sternly.

The captain said nothing, but stepped out into the corridor to speak to Mandie and Celia. "Do you girls know the boy in question?" he asked simply.

Before they could answer him, Mrs. Taft came to their rescue. She put an arm around each of them and directed them down the corridor. Senator Morton was close behind. Suddenly inspired, she turned to call back to the captain, "If you do find the boy, I strongly advise you not to make any trouble for him."

The captain stood alone in the doorway of the sick bay, dumbfounded. The strange woman had made a quick escape in the opposite direction.

As they all headed back to their cabins, Mandie wondered if they would see Jonathan again before they docked in London. She wished she hadn't had to promise not to see him again. How would they collect the reward money he had promised them? They didn't have a name or an address at which to contact him once they left the ship.

Mandie and Celia discussed the situation that night after they climbed into their bunks. Snowball curled up with Celia. He'd apparently had enough of the height of Mandie's bed.

After they turned out the light, Mandie stared out into the darkness. "Celia, we've got to figure out some way to find Jonathan after we dock."

"Yes, and soon," Celia agreed.

"Do you realize that the captain just may find him after all?" Mandie's voice quavered. "Now that he knows there's a stowaway on this ship, he'll probably have it searched from one end to the other."

Celia suddenly wondered what would happen if Jonathan was found. "What do they do with stowaways?" she asked.

"Put them in jail?" Mandie replied. Suddenly the thought of it made her sick. "Wouldn't that be awful?"

"Poor Jonathan," Celia sighed.

"Celia, I've got to talk to my grandmother tomorrow," Mandie decided. "We can't let Jonathan go to jail—not even if it means breaking our promise and telling Grandmother who he is. I really doubt the captain would put Mr. Jonathan Lindall Guyer's son in jail!"

Chapter 12 / Mysterious Message

As the ship neared port in London, the girls' excitement grew. They had to repack everything except what they would need just before the ship docked.

Charles, the handsome steward, kept them informed about the schedule.

Mrs. Taft stayed so busy with last-minute events on the ship that the girls were unable to catch her alone to talk to her about who Jonathan was. They continued to keep an eye out for him, but kept their promise not to actually go searching for him.

As they sat on the deck, Mandie talked to Celia about her frustrations. "I've just got to catch Grandmother alone," she said. "I don't want to talk to her in front of Senator Morton, but he sticks by her side like molasses all the time. And they stay up so late at night!"

Celia laughed. "Sooner or later your grandmother has to stay in her cabin long enough to repack her belongings," she reminded her. "You can catch her then."

"I hope so." Getting up from her deck chair, Mandie walked over to the rail and looked out across the churning green water. Celia joined her. "Just think," Mandie said.

"London, England, is right out there somewhere."

"I wonder how far out we'll be able to see it," Celia mused. She leaned on the rail, then glancing down at the turbulent waters below, she quickly stepped back.

Mandie smiled at her friend. "Still afraid of heights, I see. Remember when we climbed up into the belfry in that church, and you got rubbery legs?"

"I won't ever forget," Celia answered. "Swinging around on a rope way up in the air like that is the most horrible feeling I think I've ever had."

Mandie stood there for a moment, deep in thought. "I'm glad you came to the same school I did and that we got to be roommates," she said. "We've had some great times together, haven't we?"

Celia smiled. "And some bad times, too," she replied, "like when we got suspended from school for breaking curfew."

"You know, I think we're finally growing up, don't you?" Mandie turned around and leaned against the rail. "You were thirteen on March the first, and I had my thirteenth birthday on June the sixth. I suppose we'll be grown-up young ladies by the time we're sixteen, and that isn't very far off."

Celia shook her head. "Oh, I doubt it. We'll probably still be getting mixed up in all kinds of adventures. It seems to be a part of us everywhere we go."

"Whether Joe's with us or not." Mandie laughed. Just then the ship lurched and the girls grasped the railing.

"I don't think Joe would like Jonathan," Celia remarked.

"Oh, why not?"

"Because he's jealous!" Celia replied with a smirk. "He doesn't want you to have any other boys for friends."

Mandie sighed. "I know. I've fussed at him a lot about that," she said. Looking around the deck, she tried to think of something else to do. "Let's go visit Lily and Violet," she said. "We said we'd see them again before we docked."

"Sounds good," Celia agreed.

When they entered the sick bay, Violet was up, sitting in Lily's lap as Lily read to her. They were both delighted to see Mandie and Celia.

"Come in," Lily welcomed them. "I'm so glad you came again. Sit down."

As the girls sat in some comfortable chairs nearby, Violet rocked back and forth in her sister's lap. "We had company," she told them.

"You did?" Mandie replied.

"Yes, Mrs. Taft came to see us again," Lily explained.

Mandie looked surprised. "Really? My grandmother came by?"

"You just missed her," Lily answered. "She stayed with us awhile. We talked about where we will all be going once we get off this ship. She said she might bring you and Celia to my aunt's house to see us."

"That would be great!" Mandie exclaimed. "Was the senator with her?"

"No, she was alone," Lily said. "The captain had just left before she came. He's been coming in regularly. He knows the boy who saved Violet is the stowaway, so I imagine he thinks he'll catch him in here, if he comes often enough."

"Has the boy been back to visit Violet?" Mandie asked eagerly.

"No, I haven't seen him since he disappeared from here the first time," Lily replied. "The captain, your grandmother, and the doctor, of course, are the only ones who ever come to see us. The steward brings our food, but he never says anything. So we're very glad to see you two."

"I've been trying to catch my grandmother alone," Mandie explained. "I have something important I want to talk to her about, and Senator Morton is always with her."

"If she comes back before we dock, I'll tell her," Lily promised. "Oh, I almost forgot. We did have another visitor. The man who owns a newspaper in New York came by and said he'd like to write a story about Violet for his paper. He wanted to know if we had seen the boy lately."

Mandie's forehead wrinkled in concern. "He did?" She knew the newspaperman would put two and two together if the captain told him there was a stowaway on the ship. He would figure immediately that the boy was Jonathan Lindall Guyer, the third.

Lily continued, "Of course he wanted to interview the boy, too, but I told him I hadn't seen him since he ran off the first day you brought him in here." Lily looked down at her little sister, who was asleep in her arms. "Let me put her in her cot, so she'll be more comfortable."

As Lily stood, she caught her breath. "I just saw that woman in the hallway who argued with Mrs. Taft and the captain," she whispered.

Mandie stepped quickly outside to confront her. "What is it that you want?" she demanded.

The woman stood her ground and said nonchalantly, "I just want to see that you and your friend behave like young ladies on this ship." She forced a smile, then hurried off down the passageway.

"Well!" Mandie said indignantly. "She has her nerve! Did y'all hear that? She wants to see that we act like young ladies. What does she think we've been doing?"

"And what business is it of hers?" Lily asked.

Celia shook her head slowly. "I don't believe that woman is quite right," she said.

"She acts deranged," Lily agreed.

"I'll be glad when we get off this ship, so we'll be rid of her and she can't follow us around anymore!" Mandie declared.

"But we don't know where she's going, Mandie," Celia reminded her. "She may be staying in the same place we are—the Majestic Hotel."

"That's right!" Mandie gasped and covered her mouth. "I almost forgot about that note we found with 'Majestic Hotel' written on it. Do you think we'll ever get rid of her?"

"If you don't, you'll just have to ignore her," Lily suggested.

"We try to," Celia told her. "But she turns up everywhere we go."

"She seems to be out to make trouble for us," Mandie added.

"Did you say your grandmother knows her?" Lily asked.

"No," Mandie replied. "But speaking of my grandmother—Celia, let's go see if we can catch her alone."

They bade Lily goodbye with a promise to see her again.

As the girls hurried down the corridor in search of Mrs. Taft, they almost collided with Jonathan. He had just retrieved his valise from the hall closet. At the same moment, Mrs. Taft came down the hall from the opposite direction.

"Jonathan!" the girls shrieked.

Mrs. Taft caught up with them, a worried look on her face. "This boy's name is Jonathan?" she asked.

"Yes, Grandmother," Mandie admitted. "I've been trying to find a moment alone with you to tell you that this is Jonathan Lindall Guyer, the third. He is on his way to visit his aunt and uncle in Paris."

Jonathan dropped his valise to the floor. "Oh, please, you said you wouldn't tell," he groaned.

"Don't worry. My grandmother won't tell the captain, will you Grandmother?"

Before she could answer, Captain Montrose appeared suddenly from around the corner. "What was that?" he bellowed. "You mentioned the 'captain'?" He looked from Jonathan to the valise on the floor.

Everyone was speechless, and Mandie held her breath, her heart pounding.

The captain looked deeply into Jonathan's dark eyes. "Who are you, anyway?" he demanded. "I don't remember seeing you before on this voyage."

Mrs. Taft took over. "This is the boy who saved the child who fell overboard," she explained. "You did want to see him, if I recall."

Captain Montrose caught his breath. "Yes, I did." He grabbed Jonathan by the wrist. "You are coming with me to the brig. You have broken the law by stowing away on my ship."

Mrs. Taft intercepted them, touching the captain's arm. "You should know who he really is," she said. "This is none other than Jonathan Lindall Guyer, the third!"

The captain scowled. "I don't care who he is! He has broken the law, and I'm going to lock him up until we reach London. From there, the police can take over."

Mandie grasped Jonathan's other hand. "You can't

do that," she protested. "We're not going to let you."

"Let me?" Captain Montrose laughed. "My dear, young lady, I am the captain of this ship!"

Mrs. Taft spoke again. "Only until the ship docks in London," she said evenly. "Then you will be relieved of your duties with my ship line."

"*Your* ship line?" The captain almost choked. "Since when did this become *your* ship line?"

"I advise you to contact your head office on the wireless immediately," she ordered. "Find out for yourself who owns this line and whose family has owned it for over a hundred years."

The captain's face reddened and he took a step back. "I ... I'm ... terribly sorry, Mrs. Taft," he apologized. "I never connected your name with the company, even though it is the same as the company's owner. I'm truly sorry for my oversight."

At that moment Senator Morton appeared, catching the end of the conversation.

Mrs. Taft smiled at him. "We have finally located the boy who rescued Violet. And do you know who this boy's father is? The New York multimillionaire, Jonathan Lindall Guyer, the second!" she emphasized.

The senator turned to Jonathan. "*You* are Lindall Guyer's son? We'll have to let him know you've been found."

"Oh no, Senator Morton," Mandie said quickly. "Please don't do that. He's on his way to his aunt and uncle's home in Paris, and we promised to keep it a secret."

"Amanda!" Mrs. Taft exclaimed.

The senator rested his hand on Mrs. Taft's shoulder. "Your granddaughter may be right," he said, "after what we've heard about his home situation. Maybe we should at least wait until we dock."

The captain spoke up, suddenly siding with Mandie. "You may rest assured, Miss Amanda, that I will not inform his father or anyone else if that is what you wish," he said.

"Neither will I," Senator Morton agreed firmly. "In fact, I occupy a double cabin, son, and you can come share it with me. I'll even pay your fare."

"Oh—thank you, sir," Jonathan gasped, tears in his eyes.

Captain Montrose excused himself and retreated quickly down the corridor.

"Of course, Jonathan," the senator added, "there is one condition for my not informing your father. You will have to stay in our care when the boat docks until we can see what arrangements your father wants to make. He will have to be told when we get to London."

Jonathan sighed, but nodded. "All right, sir," he conceded. "I'm not in any position to ask any favors. I sincerely thank you for your generosity and kindness."

The girls looked at each other and smiled, very pleased with the turn of events.

"Jonathan," Mandie said, "I think it's great that you'll be staying with all of us. You did say you know your way around Europe, so you can show us everything!"

Mrs. Taft hugged the boy spontaneously. "We will be glad to have you, Jonathan," she said. "I may not be a particular friend of your father's, but I think he has a very nice son."

"Why, thank you, ma'am." Jonathan smiled up at her.

"Senator," Mrs. Taft turned to him. "I need a moment alone with my granddaughter. Will you see Jonathan to the dining room?" She smiled. "And thank you for taking the boy in."

Senator Morton nodded, and led the way to his room.

Mrs. Taft took the girls into her cabin and asked them to sit down. "Now, I want to make something perfectly clear," she said firmly. "Having Jonathan with us will be a completely different situation than we had planned, and I will not tolerate any secrets or unladylike behavior on your part after we get off this boat tomorrow. Is that clear?"

She took a deep breath and continued, "I will not have my visit to Europe spoiled because of two young ladies bent on foolishness, and having a good time. Any deviation from the strictest rules of ladylike behavior will not be tolerated. And if I have to speak to either of you about this again, it will be the last trip we ever make together."

The girls sat wide-eyed, a bit surprised at Mrs. Taft's outburst, but relieved that she did not seem to be overly upset about the fact that Jonathan would be accompanying them until his father could be reached.

Mandie finally found her voice and answered, "Yes, ma'am, we will not disappoint you."

"Now—" Mrs. Taft brightened. "Let's see how pretty you girls can make yourselves for dinner," she said.

"Yes, ma'am," the girls chimed in unison, relieved the conversation was over.

As they entered their own room, Mandie smiled. "We'll be ready in no time, Grandmother."

Once she shut the door, Mandie leaned against it and looked up. "Oh, thank you, God, for taking care of Jonathan," she said.

———

The next morning the passengers were informed they would dock in London that evening, after dark. The girls were too excited to eat much all day. They kept running out onto the deck to see if they could catch sight of any land. And with the pressure off to keep Jonathan's identity a secret, they could really look forward to their stay in London.

After dinner Jonathan, who looked like a different boy since he'd stayed in the senator's cabin, and was able to bathe and change his clothes, joined the girls at the rail. Mrs. Taft and Senator Morton were close by. Suddenly the ship's horn sounded loud and clear in the warm summer air.

Mandie jumped, startled by the sudden blast. She held her squirming kitten tighter in her arms.

"They've spotted land!" Jonathan said excitedly. "That's what it means when they sound the horn."

The girls hugged each other and would have danced around the deck for joy, if Mrs. Taft hadn't been there watching for ladylike behavior. The full moon was lighting up the deck, but they couldn't see very far ahead in the gathering darkness.

Mandie looked around. "I wonder where Lily and Violet are," she said. "I hope we see them before we disembark."

"Oh, dear," Mrs. Taft spoke up. "They had to go down to the steerage section to get their luggage. I did promise them we would stop by their aunt's house for a visit while we're in London. I understand she lives clear out in the countryside."

"Thank you, Grandmother," Mandie said; "that will be so much fun!"

By now most all the passengers were out on deck, and it was getting difficult to move around. The girls were glad they had come out early, so that they had a place at the railing.

Suddenly Celia squealed, pointing. "I see lights!"

Mandie peered ahead, barely able to make out the faint lights in the distance. "It's so dark," she said, squinting. "How will we ever find the hotel?"

"There are public carriages to rent that take you to the hotel," Jonathan explained. "The Majestic Hotel is quite a distance from the dock."

"You know where it is?" Mandie asked.

"Well, I've seen it. I've never stayed there," he replied. "Remember, I've always lived in schools when I've been in England."

As they gazed, wide-eyed, the lights grew bigger. The ship's foghorn sounded again and again, as they slowly reached the harbor and the ship finally pulled into dock. The gangplank lowered and people bustled forward, everyone talking excitedly.

Snowball's claws dug into Mandie's blouse. The crowd seemed to make him nervous.

Mandie was too excited about getting to London to scold the kitten. "Am I dreaming? Pinch me!" she said to Celia.

Celia pinched her, and Mandie pinched her back. "No, we're not dreaming," they said together, giggling.

"All right, girls," Mrs. Taft said. "Let's conduct ourselves as young ladies now, not children."

"Yes, ma'am," Mandie nodded, smiling at Celia.

Having moved to the top of the gangplank, everyone waited for a chain to be lowered so they could descend.

The captain held a lantern, ready to bid farewell to the passengers.

Suddenly there was a stirring and commotion in the crowd. Someone was coming up the gangplank, waving a piece of paper. It was too dark to tell who it was, but Mandie could hear the man speak to the captain.

"I have a message here for Miss Amanda Shaw."

Mandie caught her name, and without thinking she called out to the captain. "I'm right here, Captain Montrose!"

The captain took the paper from the messenger and brought it to Mandie. "A message for you, Miss Shaw."

Mandie squinted in the dim light. "It's too dark to read," she protested.

The captain held his lantern high for her.

Mandie's grandmother and the senator moved closer as Mandie read aloud. "Miss Amanda Shaw, please stop by the telegraph office. We have a message for you." She looked up, puzzled. "That's all it says." She looked at her grandmother as the captain moved away.

Mrs. Taft spoke to him as he left, "You will be hearing from us, Captain Montrose."

"Yes, ma'am," the captain replied.

Turning to Mandie, she said. "We'll stop by the telegraph office on the way to the hotel."

"But Grandmother, who would be sending me a message?"

"I have no idea, dear. We'll soon see. Let's move ahead now. The chain is down, and everyone is getting off the ship."

Mandie joined Celia and Jonathan. Senator Morton took Mrs. Taft's hand and they followed close behind.

Reaching the pier, Mrs. Taft gathered the young people to one side, while the senator went to see about the luggage and a public carriage.

Mandie was preoccupied with the mysterious message. "Where is this telegraph office, Grandmother?" she asked. Holding the ever-squirming Snowball tightly, she put the piece of paper in her handbag.

"It's a good idea to put the message in a safe place," Mrs. Taft told her. "The telegraph office is right on our way to the hotel. For the life of me, I can't think of anyone who would send you a message either."

"It couldn't be my mother or Uncle John," Mandie reasoned. "They'd send a message to you, Grandmother, not me. Isn't it expensive to send a message all the way across the ocean?"

"Yes it is," Jonathan answered her.

Mandie was so concerned, she didn't even notice anything along the way to the telegraph office in the public carriage.

Who would know where she was? Who would send a message all the way to Europe for her? What could the message be? It must be very important.

She had finally arrived in Europe to begin an exciting vacation, and someone had to add mystery to it by sending her a message!